THE WINTER

Benjamin Sturdy

authorHOUSE°

AuthorHouse™
1663 Liberty Drive
Bloomington, IN 47403
www.authorhouse.com
Phone: 1 (800) 839-8640

Published by AuthorHouse 09/24/2016

ISBN: 978-1-5246-2731-7 (sc)
ISBN: 978-1-5246-2729-4 (hc)
ISBN: 978-1-5246-2730-0 (e)

Library of Congress Control Number: 2016914361

Print information available on the last page.

To Uncle John, Aunt Sue, and Sophie

CONTENTS

PART 1

PROLOGUE

"Sir, someone's taken over the lead ship," the captain of the cargo ship yelled to the man in back of him. "They're headed for Frozer, not Vulcan. What should we do?"

"Follow the lead ship, no matter what," the man answered. "I got orders from the commander himself. Follow that ship, no matter what happens."

"But, sir, all there is on that planet is a Nova Guard base," the captain cried. "What would they do with our cargo?"

"Fleet 404's cargo could still be destroyed on Frozer," the man responded. "That's what we want. Now, the commander is on the lead ship and knows what he is doing. And don't bring up the fact that Frozer has only one atmosphere, the exosphere. We will still be able to land safely."

As the ships entered the exosphere, the captain of the ship saw that the front of the lead ship was on fire. But the fire was … different. It was the type of fire one sees when entering the atmosphere too fast.

"Sir, please—give me the command to pull up and release the parachutes!" the captain pleaded.

"No!" the man yelled. "If this is what the commander wanted, then so be it."

"*Sir, please!*" the captain screamed.

But before the man could tell the captain to calm down, it was too late.

The only *person* who survived the crash of Fleet 404 was the young commander, Peter Rack. He had grabbed one of the artifacts from the cargo hold and jumped from the ship almost a second before it hit the ground. The commander would remain on the planet for now.

He walked over to the crater left by the remains of the fleet. The snow quickly started filling in the crater. He wanted to go and find the Nova Guard base nearby, but when he saw the shock wave from the explosion, he knew it was too late. The base probably lay in ruins. He said aloud to himself, "I wonder if I will be back on Earth in time for the forming of the last golden sword."

Little did he know that some *thing* had also survived the direct crash, and that *thing* was now convinced that the commander had purposely crashed the fleet. The thing had burns all over its body, and its leg was half off. It sensed that the commander had lived and was somewhere on the planet. It yelled aloud, "Peter Rack, I will have my revenge!"

CHAPTER 1
The Unexpected

Thirty years after the crash of Fleet 404

Tomas could see only a few feet in front of him. He kept walking in a straight line, thinking he would find his way back to his father's camp. As he was walking, he fell into a seven-foot-deep hole, hitting the snowy ground with a thud. After twenty minutes of failing to get out, he tried to call for rescue.

"Help!" he yelled again and again, but no one answered.

His father had brought him on one of his archaeology trips to a planet that was always engulfed in a massive snowstorm. His father was here to look for a fleet of ships that had once carried valuable cargo but had mistaken this planet for another and crashed.

Tomas called out again.

"Tomas, is that you? Where are you?" a voice called from not far away.

"Dad, I'm stuck. Help!"

"I'm coming!" his father yelled.

The end of a rope dropped down and landed right next to Tomas. As he started to climb, something shiny caught his eye. Upon closer inspection, he saw that a piece of metal stuck out from the side of the hole.

"Wait," Tomas said.

"No, Tomas," his father demanded from above.

"Why? I just saw a piece—"

"Because some Check soldiers have found our camp and will be coming back on scoots soon."

"I thought no one lived here. It's twenty below during the day and forty below during the night. This place is completely uninhabitable."

"I know," his father remarked. "Let's just hope they aren't already at the camp."

Once Tomas was out of the hole, his father took him over to his speeder, a small hovercraft fit for five people. Once they reached the camp, he saw that all of his father's workers had already boarded the giant ship that Tomas's father used for all his excursions. The roar of engines was getting closer to them. By the sound of it, there were a lot of Check soldiers on their six-blaster scoots speeding toward them.

"Quickly, Tomas, board the ship."

Tomas watched as his father boarded the ship. He had left behind only the unimportant things, like his speeder. "What about the tents?" Tomas complained.

"Those are not as important as the food and gas," his father panted, leaning over with his hands on his knees. As soon as Tomas boarded the ship, the doors slammed behind him. The ship hovered and took off. Tomas heard the sound of gunfire.

"What do they want with us?" Tomas asked.

"Tomas, there's something I have to tell you." The ship started to rumble. "We're hit," his father murmured.

"What is it, Dad? Why do they want us?"

"Years ago, I accidentally injured a trooper on patrol. I was hunting with a friend, when suddenly something ran right by the animal I was stalking. I shot it in the hip. I thought I'd hit the animal, but by this point, the animal was long gone. There I was, looking at a motionless body. Well, it turned out that that trooper on patrol was a very highly ranked soldier in the Astro Army and was in line to become a general. My friend and I took him back to a nearby Astro Army camp. The trooper survived the accident, and once he became general, he started hunting my friend and me. He even assembled his own army, which kept growing and turned into the Check Army. Now it has about three billion soldiers stationed all across the Milky Way and Andromeda galaxies."

Tomas couldn't believe it. His father was the reason the Check Army had been formed? Suddenly Tomas heard a loud clunk on the wall behind him. His father yelled, "Run!" He grabbed Tomas's arm and ran faster than

Tomas had ever seen his father run. Tomas fell backward and tumbled down the hall of the ship, which his father had run up. A loud crash came from behind him, from where he'd heard the clunk. Tomas felt a cool breeze against his face and realized that the troops on the ground had shot some kind of device onto the door and then yanked it off.

Before Tomas could stop himself from tumbling down the slanted hall, he was falling back to the ground, three hundred feet below, where the troopers would find him. And if they discovered he was Edward Knight's son, he would immediately be imprisoned—or worse.

Tomas hit the snow with a thud. The fall stunned him, but the snow cushioned the impact. He thought his father and the ship would come back for him, but they didn't. All Tomas heard were his dad's faint yells from the ship—and the distant sound of motors on the ground, which grew louder as they approached.

The troopers must have seen him fall. As the scoots propelled themselves closer, Tomas decided that he would have to come up with a plan—and quickly—if he wanted to ever see his father again. He figured that when one of the troops got off a scoot, he would run past the troop and hijack his scoot. There was just one problem: he didn't know how to drive one.

Tomas figured his chances were slim. He would be taken to wherever the Checks were on this planet. As one of the scoots came into sight, he heard a loud roar from the engine. *Was the trooper trying to impress him by revving the engine?* he wondered. But that was not the case. The back of the engine was smoking. And this was not normal, light gray smoke; it was a thick, black, putrid-smelling smog going in all directions. The trooper riding it quickly jumped off, and seconds later it exploded.

Tomas stood there, frozen and terrified. He had seen small fires suddenly expand a few inches, but nothing this large before. The trooper suddenly stormed toward Tomas just as the other scoots were arriving and surveying the scene. The trooper shoved Tomas to the ground and starting kicking him.

"Oww!" Tomas yelped.

"Listen up, kid. These things almost never break down, so the fact that mine exploded the minute I saw you ... well, that's not right."

He reached down to grab Tomas, but before he could, Tomas jumped up and started to run. Before he could get far, Tomas heard the trooper scream an order. "After that kid! I want him alive."

The engines fired back up, and Tomas's heart raced. He knew that if he was caught, the punishment would be brutal. His father had told him about some of the suffering that prisoners endured.

When he heard a screech up ahead, he knew what it was. His father had warned him about this before they'd come here. It was a custos, a massive two-headed snake that lived in the most unexpected places. When the troopers heard this sound, they stopped their scoots and turned around.

"You're on your own, kid," said a trooper as he turned around and moved away from Tomas. "We were looking for someone else anyway."

With that, they left. How could Tomas live through this? He knew it was the end when the hundred-foot-long white snake rose out of the ground. It had bright-blue eyes on each head, and spikes were scattered all over its body. Then he remembered the hole he'd fallen into earlier that day and the piece of metal sticking out of the side. If he could make it there alive, maybe he could see what it was. Maybe it was a door to one of the ships his father was looking for. But the hole was at least three hundred feet away, and the snake struck at him before he could formulate his plan.

The snake lunged at him, and he jumped out of the way before it could land on him. Unfortunately, one of the spikes snagged onto his coat and ripped it off, leaving a deep gash in Tomas's back. Tomas started running, but visibility was low, and he had no idea where he was going. He ran in the direction he had come from, and after about five long minutes of breathless dodging, he fell into a pit. He thought the custos had lost him, but that wasn't the case at all.

Tomas felt the snowy walls for a few seconds until he felt heavy breathing over him. He slowly looked up to see one giant blue eye looking down at him. He searched the walls frantically until he found that piece of metal.

As he examined it, he noticed something peculiar. This was no door, he realized. And it was definitely not a piece of debris. He yanked on the metal and felt a freezing handle. As he kept pulling, he realized that it was a sword. It had a snowy-white handle, an icy, light-blue blade, and a tiny glass ball near the handle.

Tomas looked up at the giant eye staring down at him. The snake lifted its heads and stared at the sword in Tomas's outstretched hand. It seemed mesmerized. And then the snake vanished. In disbelief, Tomas looked down at his shaking hand that held the sword. What had just happened?

Tomas dropped the sword when he saw where the custos had gone. The tiny ball at the bottom of the sword was glowing, and inside it was a very small version of the snake slithering around.

Now Tomas had another problem to face. How would he get out of this hole? He tried scaling the wall. He tried using his new sword as a shovel. None of these techniques worked. The sun was going down, and he knew he couldn't survive the night. He was not in a heated tent, and he had only a light jacket on. He tried jumping up and down to warm himself. He was astonished to find that he had jumped straight out of the hole— and even higher. He also landed like a feather. What was with this sword?

As he started walking toward the camp his father had left behind, he noticed the large pieces of a ship that had been destroyed in the crash thirty yeas ago, lying in the snow. Tomas ignored it, and then noticed something inscribed on the blade: "It has chosen you. You are now its owner. You will use it appropriately. Be warned. You are the one *They* want."

What did it mean by "*They*"? Tomas didn't want to be chosen. He had never used or even held a weapon. If what it said was true, he had now been warned that *They* wanted him, and his only hope was to teach himself how to use this sword "appropriately." He decided to sleep on the idea in a heated tent, though he was afraid he might not have until morning.

Tomas kept waking up throughout the night. He was afraid that whatever was coming for him would find him and most likely kill him, because the words on the sword said, "*They* want."

When the sun rose in the morning, Tomas got some supplies his father had left behind to build a fire. He did this so that if any people lived close by, they would be able to see the smoke and maybe come and investigate. When it was about noon, the fire had burned itself out, and Tomas has become very hungry. He figured that if he didn't eat for another few days, he would die. He wasn't worried about water, though, because all he could see was snow for miles.

Tomas decided to explore the site where he'd found the sword. Maybe the missing ships his father was looking for were in that area. And maybe there would be supplies or, even better, food. After an hour of digging small holes and looking for ships or anything edible, Tomas kept thinking about the sword and its purpose. He came to the conclusion that someone had created the sword and hid it—or lost it. He didn't know why he thought this. It just seemed like a reasonable explanation.

When the sun was going down, it started to get windy. Tomas knew it was time to head into his tent. Suddenly the little version of the custos started to glow yellow. At that very moment, a figure appeared from a gust of wind. He had pale skin, long dark hair tied into a bun, and a beard. He carried what looked like an exact replica of Tomas's sword, except that the handle was dark green, not snowy white.

"Hello," the man called from about thirty feet away. "Are you lost?" His voice was deep and hearty. "I found you because my custos ball was glowing. When a sword is close to another sword, they glow yellow. All I had to do was keep going in this direction, and here we are."

Tomas had trouble responding. He was just so shocked that someone had found him. Then he noticed a huge scar from a beast on the man's face. "No ... well, I kind of am," he finally managed to respond.

"Name's Peter Rack, but you can call me Pete." There was a long pause, and then Pete said, "If you want, you can stay at my—"

Before he could finish, Tomas asked, "How did you get that sword? Does everyone have them on this planet?" Tomas felt bad for interrupting him, but he couldn't wait to find out. The question had been burning inside of him since the moment he saw that Pete had a sword.

"Oh, this?" Pete asked, pointing at the sword and sounding surprised. "It's the one thing I managed to hold on to when Fleet 404 crashed here many years ago. All the ships had hundreds of these on them. They were forged from stars all across the Andromeda galaxy, and they had unimaginable powers. They were created to keep peace in the galaxies, but instead, wars were fought over them. Their creators had given them out to peacekeepers, people who pledged their lives to protecting the galaxies from evil. Eventually, though, the power corrupted them, and they turned them against each other. Over the years, many have been lost or destroyed. That was when the Nova Guard was created. They tracked down the remaining swords for hundreds of years and were supposed to take them to Vulcan, the planet next to this one. There the ships were supposed to destroy the remaining swords in the lava.

"But somehow they mistook a red planet for a blue planet. I was on board one of the ships when this happened, and I grabbed a sword and jumped. I broke my collarbone in the fall, but it was worth it. I've managed to live here for thirty years by hunting wild animals. When the fleet crashed by accident, some of the small creatures called … um … I forget. Well, they are big now, after escaping from the little glass balls they lived in, and they've been roaming around ever since."

Tomas looked at Pete in awe and amazement.

"Come on, kid. You can stay at my place tonight," Pete said. "I never caught your name."

Tomas was astonished. Pete hadn't asked how Tomas had gotten his sword or even how he'd gotten on this planet. But Tomas responded appropriately. "My name's Tomas Knight."

"Well, Tomas, you look hungry. How about a bowl of polar bear soup?"

Tomas nodded his head in agreement, even though the thought of polar bear soup sounded gross. "Sure," he said, and they both walked off together, clutching their glowing swords.

When they reached Pete's house, Tomas was surprised. He had not expected an igloo. This one was rectangular with a dome roof. The entrance was a piece of metal that had dents and scrapes all over it.

"How long have you been here?" Pete asked.

"About twenty-four hours." Tomas decided not to tell Pete about the Checks being after his father, because he didn't know if Pete was working for the Checks. Even though it seemed very unlikely, his father had once said that anything is possible. As Pete pulled the piece of metal away from the doorway, Tomas looked inside to see chairs, a bed, and even a boiler connected to a heater. There were also what looked like a toilet, a table, and a stove.

Tomas had been expecting something very plain, with maybe a pillow and a table, but not this.

"Where did you get all this stuff?" Tomas somehow blurted out.

"When Fleet 404 crashed, I managed to locate the remains of some ships before they were covered in snow, and I found some stuff that had not been burned."

Tomas walked slowly into Pete's igloo and noticed even more stuff inside. There was a bookshelf leaning up against a wall, and it had some small rocks scattered on the shelves. There was also a bow with about thirty arrows lying in back of Pete's bed—and lots more.

"Wait," said Tomas. "If you've lived here thirty years, and you hunt animals outside, and you don't have much clothing—well, I mean, like coats—and the average temperature is usually minus-twenty degrees, then how come you've managed to live so long?"

Pete answered, "Well, the first ten years were hard. My body was not used to such extreme conditions, mainly because I'm from a place called Earth. But my body adjusted to the cold after a while, and soon it felt natural."

Tomas had heard the name *Earth* before, but didn't know a lot about it. "Isn't Earth one of Jupiter's moons?"

Pete started to laugh. "No!" he bellowed. "It's the third planet from that fireball … well, on Earth they called it the *sun*. You should know more about Earth, Tomas. After all, it's where human life began."

There was a long pause, and suddenly Pete said, "Oh, right, polar bear soup." He quickly ran over to another piece of metal—a trap door in the ground—and opened it and hopped down.

Tomas felt sick when Pete came out of the compartment with a polar bear's arm. Pete could tell that Tomas was looking a little queasy and finally said, "Oh this, this is for me. Your soup is up on top of the heater." Tomas was shocked to see Pete roast and eat the arm so quickly.

After about five minutes of eating, Tomas asked, "Do you know who *They* are?"

Pete looked up from his meal "Who? The polar bears? Yeah, I know them."

"No, not that," Tomas murmured. "I mean on the sword. It says, 'Be warned. You are the one *They* want.'"

Pete looked down at his sword and picked it up. His eyes widened, and then he said, "Oh, I never noticed that. *They*. There are these guys dressed in black robes, who have their own swords. They used to be peacekeepers, but their swords' power took over their bodies. The swords also kept them from dying."

"Have you ever encountered a peacekeeper?" Tomas asked.

"I encounter a group of them about every few weeks. They are not that hard to fight off … well, if you know how to use a sword."

Tomas thought about this for a while and then asked, "What do they do with the swords if they, well, um …"

"Kill you?" Pete shrugged with a frown. "Beats me."

After Tomas finished his soup, which was surprisingly good, Pete set up a sleeping bag he somehow had and gave Tomas his bed. "We can talk more in the morning," Pete said with sadness in his voice.

"Okay." Tomas nodded, and they both went to sleep, but not for long.

Pete woke Tomas up at about midnight, breathing heavily from his mouth. "Listen, Tomas. I need you to hide in my freezer—where I pulled out the polar bear's arm. Just stay in there until I come back."

"Why?" Tomas asked, frightened.

"I'll explain later. Just stay in the freezer."

Tomas ran over to the piece of metal in the floor, opened it, and jumped in. After Pete put the metal back in place, Tomas heard the sound of snow being piled on top of it. Tomas was left in utter darkness, alone. His heart was racing. His whole body was trembling with fear.

Suddenly, he heard the sound of people marching right above him. Then he heard yells, followed by the sound of engines and the buzzing sound of a 42-blaster warming up. Tomas knew what 42-blasters were used for: making things explode. Whatever was happening, Pete would not be able to live through it.

Tomas jumped up and lunged, hands-first, into the piece of metal. It flew up into the air, and the snow piled over it went everywhere. Tomas went to where he'd hidden his sword, only to find out that it was gone. Furious that Pete had taken his sword without asking, Tomas stomped toward the door. Before he could kick it down and take his sword back from Pete, he realized that Pete had just taken the burden of the powerful sword off his shoulders. This meant that the crazy peacekeepers would not look for him anymore. He was free of fear. But then he remembered something important.

He was going to disobey Pete's commands and go out there and save him.

This time Tomas walked toward the door, not in anger but with pride. He ran right into it and knocked it down. When he knocked it down, he heard what sounded like something heavy landing on the snow. Tomas slowly looked down and then around him. Three hundred Check soldiers surrounded the igloo—some on scoots, some on foot, and some mounted on 42-blasters. Then he noticed Pete with a gash on his forehead and some rips in his coat. He looked in Pete's hands and saw his green-handled sword. Suddenly, Tomas fell to the ground.

A few feet behind him, the igloo burst into pieces of stone, wood, polar bear, and of course, lots of snow. The 42-blaster had gone off, making no noise at all but producing a silent shock wave. Once Pete and all the other troopers got up, Tomas was surrounded by them. Between them, Tomas saw something amazing. Pete held the sword upside down and then jabbed it into the snow. About a second before this happened, Pete yelled, "Jump, Tomas!"

Tomas did as he was told and jumped. At that same moment, the ground turned lightning-blue and then sank. Tomas felt himself falling, but he soon felt snow. He was on a snow mound. He looked off the edge of the mound and noticed that there were holes going down into blackness. His mound was at ground level. Pete's mound was about fifteen feet away.

"What just happened?" Tomas screamed.

"I just created a sinkhole, but the real question is why you came out of there," Pete said casually.

"I heard what sounded like an entire army, with 42-blasters and scoots. Besides, if I'd stayed in there, I would have died."

Suddenly, the snow was back in its place, the holes filled in. But the troops had vanished. Tomas stared, mesmerized by the scene.

Pete said, "Tomas, go find your sword. Then follow me."

Before Tomas went looking for his sword, he said, "It's still midnight. Can't we wait until morning?"

"No!" Pete snapped. "Find your sword and just follow me."

"Pete, my sword wasn't in the igloo when I looked for it. Did you move it?" Tomas asked.

"Yeah, sorry. I thought it was mine when the Checks showed up, until I realized mine was tucked into my belt, so I tossed it into the bookshelf."

Tomas looked around the remains of Pete's igloo and eventually saw the sword lying in the snow. As Tomas started to walk towards it, a loud roar broke the midnight silence.

"Scoots," Tomas whispered to Pete, but Pete was already running away. "Follow me," he barked.

After about twenty minutes of running, Pete stopped. He took a button out of his coat pocket and pressed it. The ground started to shake, and about five feet in front of Tomas, something that seemed like a giant wall rose from the ground. Pete circled the giant box and then opened something. It was a massive door, and inside was a B-230 spacecraft. Written on the side was "NOVA GUARD."

"Why haven't you left this place before?" Tomas asked softly.

"Because," Pete said. "Where would I go? I don't need to be back on Earth for another … ten hours. I'm also a lot safer here than another planet."

The craft had four wings, all folded up into a small rectangle. They were attached to a hexagon, which was attached to an oval cockpit. Pete flipped open the cockpit and said, "Quickly, get in."

Tomas climbed into the small cockpit to notice that there were two leather seats, one facing toward the cockpit window, and one facing toward the wall. Tomas knew he was supposed to sit in the second leather seat, the one facing the wall. After he'd sat down and buckled himself in, Pete came and opened the wall up, almost like he was opening a trailer, starting at the bottom and pulling up.

Tomas's chair zoomed forward and then came to an instant stop, giving him minor whiplash. That was when he figured out what he was going to do on this voyage. In front of him, a square window attached to a blaster lay motionless, but not for long.

"How did this get here?" Tomas asked in wonder.

"I found it here," Pete said.

"How? Did the Nova Guard create some kind of base here?"

"They did, in fact," Pete said.

Tomas tried moving the blaster around, which was surprisingly light, and accidently fired it at the wall.

"Okay, Tomas, just don't touch it until I tell you to. Got it?"

"Got it."

Suddenly, the roof to the bunker opened, and Tomas noticed that they were lifting off the ground.

"How does this run?" Tomas asked, knowing that fuel could not last very long in a single fuel tank.

"Solar energy. Back on Earth I flew these crafts around all the time. They are programmed to go faster on the equinox or solstice. And today just happens to be the vernal equinox."

Tomas was not paying attention to Pete anymore. When he looked down, he saw more than just a few scoots; he saw hundreds. His heart stopped when he saw one of them take out a telamonotor, a far-ranging walkie-talkie used to make contact with vessels in space. This meant that the Check army was waiting for them outside the planet's exosphere.

Pete finally said, "Hey, Tomas, remember that thing I wanted to tell you about an hour ago? Well, it was this. I was with someone named Edward Knight, and we were hunting rogars on Artemis, a planet known for hunting and having many moons. He accidently shot a soldier who was running about forty feet behind our prey. The wounded man was working for the Astro Army, and he later became general of the army. Well, he told his troops that he was starting his own army, and that if they didn't join it, he would kill them.

Soon, most of the Astro Army soldiers had joined the general's army, and the Astro Army was torn apart. The general has been hunting both of us down for years and will not stop hunting us until we are dead. He renamed the Astro Army the Check Army. So I'm bringing you to Earth, because I know you're Edward Knight's son, and if that general finds out, you're in trouble. Big trouble. And don't even get me started on Azamore and his army."

Tomas, nearly speechless after this admission, tried to ask how Pete knew that he was Edward Knight's son, but before he could form the words, Pete said, "Tomas, shooting the wall was the only training you got with the R-509 blaster, but I think I'm going to be counting on you to hit a few Check crafts if you want to be safe. Okay, stay still. I'm moving you."

"What?" Tomas asked, confused. Suddenly, a door came shooting out of a slit right above his head and curved around him. At that very moment, he felt his capsule start moving forward. *Oh,* Tomas thought, *I'm being sent off into space to hit some Check ships, and after that, Pete will come and attach me back onto his Nova vehicle. Simple.*

But that wasn't the case at all. Once his capsule was almost out of the craft, he heard a grinding noise, and then he knew he was moving around the side of the ship. Suddenly a voice came from a small box on side of the wall. It said, "Ok, Tomas, I can see out of the planet, and there's a massive blockade deploying Queen-4430's. They are easy to destroy, but they move at extremely fast speeds. Do your best. Peter, out."

Once the craft had left the atmosphere, Tomas grew slightly cold. Then Pete's Pete came from the box again. "Tomas, don't let the cold of space affect you. The cold is a different kind of cold than the cold of Frozer. It affects your muscles. Just bear with me for about four more hours."

"It's going to be a bumpy ride," Tomas murmured, and at that moment, the Queen-4430s started heading straight for them.

A Queen-4430 was not large. The cockpit was a circle, and attached to the end of it was a parachute-like sail. Tomas's face went pale, and he was overwhelmed with fear. When the first craft came within firing distance, Tomas started firing in every direction, waving the blaster around while holding down the button that said "Fire."

Pete spoke to Tomas through the speaker. "Tomas, keep it up. Your strategy seems to be working." Tomas had no idea what Pete meant. But once Tomas got a clear view of what he was doing, he was amazed. Because of his wild firing, Tomas had completely scattered the swarm of crafts, forcing them into each other. He kept on doing this until he realized that he was beginning to feel sore.

The cold had gotten to his muscles, and this made it painful to move the blaster around. He began to feel light-headed, and then his eyes became heavy. Tomas now felt as if someone had injected Novocain into his body. He could not feel anything, and he grew unaware of what was happening around him. Then, he fell asleep, right when Pete needed him.

"Tomas, I need you!" Pete yelled through the speaker. "He's asleep," Pete murmured to himself. He started thinking about how to get through the blockade. He came up with an idea, but it would be risky. He would fly his craft right through the blockade at maximum speed. Once he was beyond the blockade, he only needed to get away from the Check fleet, which he could do by flying in a straight line. Then he could swap places with Tomas, who was still asleep, and handle the blaster. It could work, but first he'd need to create a bigger mess.

Pete pressed a button that he had never thought he would have to press. The button said, "Release All Turbines." The turbines were at the ends of the wings, and since there was emergency power available, the trip would go faster without them—mainly because they weighed two tons in all. Pete watched as the turbines floated away toward the crafts and then exploded, creating a distraction. He flew right through the mix of fire and smoke, completely undetected. When he was about seven hundred feet away from the blockade, he figured he would not need to switch places with Tomas, because there was no sign of pursuit. Even though emergency power didn't make the craft any faster, it could still get them places and keep them moving.

After many hours of going at very high speeds, Pete decided to go and check on Tomas. Pete put the craft on autopilot and opened the door to Tomas's capsule. Tomas was slouched down in his chair, probably because when Pete pressed the button that brought Tomas's capsule back into the craft, it must have come in pretty fast. "Tomas," Pete whispered. "Tomas, can you hear me?"

"Mum fne," Tomas mumbled. Before he could shake out of his stupor, he dozed right off again. Pete remembered that this had happened to him the first few times he'd gone into space, but after a while, his body had adjusted to the cold.

Pete went back up to the front and saw some of the planets in the solar system they were entering. "Boy, am I hungry. Better pick up the speed." Because of the equinox today, Pete was in luck.

While flying through the solar system toward Earth, Pete noticed a massive piece of metal. He slowed down the craft when he saw that something was written on it. It said, "In loving memory of Alexia Stock, Morgan Hidenburg, Justin Mane, and Larry Robbins for their courage to try to change the course of history in 2024 by attempting to fly to Mars on Apollo 34. May they rest in peace." Pete had seen a massive memorial like this before, because there were hundreds of them floating around in the solar system. Every ten years for the past two thousand, humankind had sent one into space to remain there forever.

When Pete saw the Earth's moon, he knew he was close. Earth was advancing more and more every year, and Pete figured that there was some small token or reward he could get on Earth for Tomas for not telling him that he would fall asleep and be like he was right now.

As they passed the moon, Pete saw that the colony there had grown in the last thirty years, with skyscrapers and massive buildings inside the domes that surrounded the colony. As they entered the atmosphere, Pete heard moaning from the place where Tomas was. Pete gave a quick glance behind him to see that Tomas was standing up and stretching.

"Pete, where are we?" Tomas asked, fully awake now.

"We are in the stratosphere."

"Pete that really doesn't help. What planet are we on"

"Earth," Pete laughed. Tomas walked over to the window by Pete and saw a giant surface of water. "Welcome to the Atlantic Ocean," Pete said happily.

"Is all of Earth like this?" Tomas asked, confused.

"I think I'll let you find that out," Pete said. As the craft went forward, Tomas could see a light-green statue of someone holding a torch in one hand and a book in another, but for some reason it had no head. After the statue, Tomas saw a huge crater where the harbor should have been. After that, he saw giant buildings touching the clouds, and small crafts buzzing all over the place. "How are they not bumping into each other?" Tomas asked, amazed by the sight.

"All of the crafts have something built into them. It's called echolocation. If another craft comes within two feet of the craft, it automatically finds another way to get to get to the passenger's destination."

As they landed the Nova Guard vehicle in a "parking lot," the cockpit opened, and they both hopped out. Pete led Tomas down a white sidewalk and into a shop full of little gizmos. "Whatever you want," Pete offered, waving his hand around the room.

Tomas went looking around with a smile on his face. He eventually picked out a grappling hook. When they walked up to the cashier, the cashier said, "That will be … I'm sorry, sir. Please take it, free of charge."

Tomas put it into his pocket happily, but then saw the custos in his sword glowing yellow.

"Um, Pete," Tomas said, pointing at his custos.

"Oh, no," Pete whispered, looking at his own custos. "*They* have found us. Follow me." Pete started to run.

Tomas looked back into the crowd of people, and his heart almost stopped when he caught a glimpse of a figure in a black robe with a black hood. Then some people blocked his view, and when Tomas saw the figure again, he had a sword in his hands. The sword was completely black. Then more of the hooded figures started appearing all around the crowd, all staring directly at Tomas and Pete.

"In here," Pete said, clearly under stress. Tomas ran after Pete into a building. It was a normal building that looked like all the ones next to it.

"Why here?" Tomas asked.

"I'll explain in the elevator," Pete said.

They ran into an elevator, and Tomas watched Pete press a red button labeled "City Heating." He was confused. Was Pete going to try to burn the peacekeepers in a heater?

"I'm going to try to burn the peacekeepers in the heaters," Pete said.

"Oh," Tomas thought, wondering how that would unfold. The doors to the elevator closed, and Tomas felt a little queasy when the elevator started going down, but he got used to it after a minute or so. Then Tomas noticed something frightening. "Pete," he said, "Look at your custos."

Pete looked down, and then his mouth opened. As they were going deeper down, their custoses were getting more and more yellow.

At that moment the doors to the elevator opened, and what looked like fifty peacekeepers were waiting for them. With them were Check soldiers and a general. But this wasn't just any general. This was the general whom Tomas's father had shot, and he had a sword. Just when Tomas thought things couldn't get any worse, he saw the elevator go back up behind them. It had been their only way out of the mess they were in. They were going to have to fight their way through if they wanted to live.

The heater room was a lot larger than Tomas had expected. There were straight bridges crisscrossing throughout the open space, and next to them were a couple of heaters and boilers attached to tubes that all went upward. The room was more like a warehouse, and it had straight bridges going down the length for at least a mile. Tomas figured that there had to be another elevator shaft somewhere, but he could not see one through the mass of soldiers and peacekeepers. Pete then whispered to Tomas, "Do what I do."

Tomas whispered back, "Okay."

Pete ran forward, and Tomas—along with all of the soldiers but not peacekeepers—looked surprised. Tomas ran right behind Pete and became even more frightened when he heard the Check soldiers' guns make a clicking noise. Then, out of the corner of his eye, Tomas saw Pete's custos turn from yellow to red, and he knew something was about to happen.

Before Tomas could make any sense of what Pete was doing, Tomas felt the bridge shake violently. Tomas, along with everyone else, dropped to the ground. Tomas looked up to see Pete waving his sword, which was now glowing red as he waved it around in every direction. Tomas noticed that whichever way the sword was pointing, the bridge moved that way too.

Suddenly, the bridge became still. Tomas could not understand why until he saw all of the peacekeepers and the general waving their swords up and down or side to side. When he looked over at Pete, he saw that Pete was on the ground and crumpled into a ball. The general walked over to Pete, who was closer to him than Tomas was, and raised his sword over his head. Tomas knew what was about to happen.

Without thinking, Tomas threw his sword at the general. The general looked at him and swung his sword at Tomas's, trying to hit it like a baseball. He succeeded. The sword went flying over the edge of the bridge and down into blackness.

"Tomas!" Pete screamed. Tomas looked over at Pete and saw his sword come hurtling through the air. Tomas caught it and quickly examined it. There was something Tomas had never noticed about Pete's sword. It had a green custos. He remembered that their custoses had been the same back on Frozer—light blue. But in the middle of Tomas's thoughts, a bullet whizzed right by his face.

Tomas looked up to see that the soldiers had advanced forward, and the peacekeepers were now only five feet in front of him. Tomas still had no idea how to use the sword—until he remembered the glowing green custos. He swung the sword gently, and at that very moment, everything started to float—except Tomas.

"To make everything go down, swing the sword left and tap the glass ball holding the custos," Pete said from in the air. Tomas figured that when Pete had thrown the sword to him, he had already done something to make this happen. Pete had assumed that Tomas would swing it, and when he did, this would happen.

"Cool. Antigravity," Tomas said happily. Then he figured that if Pete didn't come down soon, he would die of impact when he did come down. Tomas waved the sword left and tapped the glass ball, and everything fell back down. Tomas ran over to Pete and helped him up.

Then Tomas heard a bang from behind. It seemed louder than any of the other sounds he'd heard. He heard a cry from Pete, who fell from Tomas's arms. Pete had been shot. Tomas looked back to see one of the peacekeepers pointing his sword at Pete.

"No!" Tomas cried. He leaped almost twenty feet at the peacekeeper, knocking him over. Tomas stood up before the peacekeeper could, and he plunged his sword into the peacekeeper's chest. Tomas did not expect that the peacekeeper would turn to dust, leaving his robes and sword in a heap on the ground. Tomas ran around the swarm of peacekeepers, slicing and stabbing them all. They all turned to dust. The remaining soldiers and peacekeepers all ran into different elevators.

"Don't think you've won, kid!" the general yelled as he retreated with the peacekeepers. "It's not over!" The general stared at Tomas as the elevator doors closed.

Tomas stood there in silence with piles of robes and swords around him. He felt his anger start cooling down. Then he remembered Pete. He ran over to Pete and knelt down next to him. "Pete," Tomas cried. "Pete, stay with me."

"I'll be okay, kid. Don't worry," Pete answered.

"But the bullet went right into your chest, right?" Tomas said, still confused as to how Pete could still be alive.

Pete unbuttoned his coat to reveal a strange-looking vest. "Laser-proof and bulletproof," Pete said proudly. "It still hurts when you're shot, but you live."

"That's a relief." Tomas sighed, frowning. "So, how are we going to get my sword?" Tomas asked Pete.

"Seriously? Look around you."

Tomas looked around him to see the many swords left by the peacekeepers. "Oh," he said. He walked over to a pile of swords with Pete. He walked over to one sword that looked interesting. It was not all black, as it had some yellow streaks all over it. Tomas asked Pete, "Do all these swords do the same thing?"

"No," Pete answered.

Then Tomas remembered that this was the sword the peacekeeper had used to shoot Pete. Tomas picked it up, and the blade turned from black with yellow streaks, to white with yellow streaks. The handle changed to yellow with white streaks on it. Even the custos changed colors. "This will do," Tomas said. Pete and Tomas walked toward the elevator that had been in back of them the entire time. "So, why exactly did we come down here?" Tomas asked.

"Because once every hundred years, a golden sword is mysteriously forged down here," Pete said. "But I guess General Ventex got here first and claimed it. I wanted to have the golden sword so I could stop the Check Army, so I guess we'll just have to get it somehow."

"Why can't we just use your sword or mine?" Tomas asked.

"Because that golden sword has the power to tear apart planets and solar systems in the blink of an eye," Pete said.

"So the reason for bringing me here was to get the sword?" Tomas asked, now a little angry.

"I'm afraid it was," Pete answered apologetically. "I'm so sorry."

"Um, when will I see my father again?" Tomas asked.

"Soon," Pete responded, "but I can't make any promises." They got into the elevator after tossing all the swords and robes down into the inky abyss below them.

Tomas asked, "Pete, who are you? I mean, there was the whole cashier thing and the Nova Guard ship."

"Tomas," Pete said nervously, "I'm not just some normal guy who owns a sword. I was a widely known commander for the Nova Guard. I was in charge of the Nova Guards patrol Earth for a few years. I earned a lot of respect from almost everbody on the planet."

That night Tomas and Pete slept in the Nova Guard craft. Tomas still couldn't believe that Pete had been a high-ranking person in the Nova Guard and that everyone seemed to know who he was. Then Tomas remembered Pete's igloo. If Pete had been living on Frozer for thirty years, how did everyone still recognize him? And when Pete had said, "Where would I go?" before they boarded the Nova Guard craft, had he meant that the Nova Guard didn't want him anymore?

Tomas decided to sleep on all his questions for the night, but after about an hour of trying to get to sleep, Tomas decided to think some more. Then he had an idea that almost made him jump. What if his father worked for the Nova Guard too? Tomas thought this because Pete had told him that his father had been hunting with him, and they had—

Before Tomas could finish his thought, he heard the sound of engines above him. The engines were too loud to be those of the Nova Guard craft they were sleeping in. Then Tomas heard Pete saying into a walkie-talkie, "How about bay five?" After a long pause, he said, "Got it." Tomas then felt the craft moving upward. Tomas ran to the cockpit and looked up to see a massive gray ship with one big star on the side.

"Pete, what's happening?" Tomas asked, scared.

"You are going to start training with the Nova Guard as a Nova knight," Pete said.

"Oh, because my last name is Knight. I get it," Tomas said cheerfully.

"No, that's not why at all." Pete said. "It's because you are going to become a real knight. The Nova Guard finds kids that are … well … different from all the others. They train these kids with those swords that you and I have, transforming them into peacekeepers—the good kind. Their job is to protect the galaxies from growing threats, like the Checks."

"How am I different?" Tomas asked.

"Because you have shown resistance to the sword's power," Pete said. "Most kids become overwhelmed with the power and become crazy."

"But I'm only fifteen," Tomas said.

Suddenly, Pete became very quiet. "Tomas, I think it's time to say our farewells," he said sadly. "You do not need me anymore." Tomas looked down at his feet. He was sad that Pete was leaving. "Don't worry. You are in good hands. And remember, if you land on the moon for any reason, don't stay for long. The moon colonies are full of murderers and thieves."

As the craft approached the ship, Tomas noticed a giant door open. Inside was a platform labeled in giant letters: "BAY 5." Pete landed the craft on a platform above the massive doors. Pete opened the cockpit door and let Tomas out. "Stay out of trouble," he said as Tomas reluctantly climbed out of the craft. Then he closed the cockpit door and waved through the glass. Tomas didn't take his eyes off the craft until he could no longer see it in the night sky. He was left alone, staring into the inky night.

Then he heard footsteps behind him. He quickly spun around to see a man in a white suit. At his side was a scrawny boy who was looking at his own feet. The man stopped about a foot in front of Tomas. He had gray hair and looked to be about seventy. "Hello, Tomas," the man said. "I'm Director Pierce. Welcome."

Tomas followed Director Pierce down a long hallway of the space ship until they got to a window. The window overlooked a large, grassy field with trees and massive rectangles in the ground. Director Pierce said, "This is our training arena. Here we send our students to play a game of Capture the Flag. The only difference between normal Capture the Flag and this one is that you use your sword to eliminate other players. There are no boundaries, meaning that you may strike someone anywhere on the field. You will begin at seven o'clock tomorrow morning. Allen will lead you to your dorm." Director Pierce pointed to the weak, brown-haired boy about Tomas's age. Allen trudged down a set of stairs to their left, and Tomas followed.

"Hi," Tomas said, not knowing what else to say.

"Hey," Allen replied immediately.

"I'm Tomas Knight," Tomas said, extending his hand.

"I'm Allen Lister," Allen said, shaking Tomas's hand.

"How long have you been here?" Tomas asked.

"About two weeks," Allen said. "Why are you here exactly?"

"I don't know," Tomas said. "One minute I'm fighting peacekeepers in a heating room with a friend, and the next I'm finding out I'm being sent into an arena to die."

"You don't die," Allen said. "Some people do this thing to your sword so it won't hurt you. I mean, it hurts, but you live. I've been in the arena twice, and it's hard, especially to capture the flag."

Tomas then asked, "Why are you here?"

"My folks passed away when I was young. Before I was sent here, I used my power for both good and bad purposes; I didn't care which. Then I found my sword, and everything changed."

"What's your skill?" Tomas asked.

"This," Allen said, stretching his arm out toward Tomas. "Now touch me."

"Um … okay," Tomas said. He reached out and tried to touch Allen, but before he could, Tomas was spinning madly in the air around him. Allen could create tornadoes with his mind.

"Stop!" Tomas yelled. Once back on the ground, Tomas was still baffled at how Allen could do this. He asked, "Can you do anything else besides create tornadoes?"

"I don't create tornadoes. I simply create an orbit. Just think of it this way: I'm a star, and you are my planets." There was a long pause, and then Allen asked, "What power do you have?"

"I don't have a power," Tomas said quietly.

"I'm sure you do. Everyone has a power. It's just that most people are always so busy doing something else that they never have time to find it. But if everyone knew how to use his own power, wars would break out, and worlds would be torn apart. So would families."

After another long pause, Allen led Tomas through a door into a room with five bunk beds and a wooden door, which Tomas guessed was the bathroom. There was also a metal pad on the floor in the middle of the room.

"You can sleep on the high bed above mine," Allen said, pointing. Tomas settled down and had a long conversation with Allen about the Nova Guard.

After their conversation, Allen said, "Okay, Tomas, act cool."

"Huh?" Tomas was confused, but before Allen had time to explain, he heard laughter outside the room. The door slammed open, and six boys appeared, all having swords in their hands except for one. Tomas heard a few words from the conversation, like *burned* and *cut up*. Tomas knew that whatever they were talking about must not be good. It must have had something to do with their training.

One of the boys looked up at Tomas and yelled, "New guy!" Then all the boys ran over to his bunk and yanked the mattress off the supporters and let it fall. Tomas hit the ground with a thud, and when he got up, he saw that the boys had surrounded him. Tomas expected to be punched or kicked, but instead they started introducing themselves.

The first boy who introduced himself had black hair and was very tall and very tan. "I'm Roger Barren," he said. The next boy who came up to Tomas and was about Tomas's height, but he had red hair and lots of freckles. "I'm Patrick Doric. Nice to meet you." The next two boys approached Tomas. They both had blond hair like Tomas, but they looked exactly the same. "I'm Teddy," said one. "And I'm Freddy," said the other. "We're twins."

"Hello," Tomas said back. The last boy approached. He was small and looked scared for some reason. "I'm Nathan Winter," he said. Then Nathan ran straight to his loft and buried himself in the covers.

"Nathan can see the future," Roger said. "He's really creepy."

Tomas noticed that Nathan had a purple sword with blue specks all over it. Freddy and Teddy both had dark-green swords with black handles. Roger had a red sword with specks of gray, and Patrick had an all-gray sword.

After Tomas had put his mattress back on the bunk bed, he heard Patrick say to Roger, "Hey, Patrick, I bet you ten units that the kid doesn't make it through the week."

"No deal, bro," Patrick said. "Bet you twenty units he makes it through the week."

"Deal," Roger said firmly.

Then Allen said, "Guys, go to bed. It's midnight."

"Okay, sunny boy," Teddy joked, making all the other boys except Nathan crack up. Tomas didn't know why this was so funny, and then remembered Allen telling him to think of him as a star. And another name for a star is the sun. Tomas couldn't help laughing a little once he understood the joke. After a few minutes he fell asleep, frightened for the day to come.

Tomas woke up early. He looked at the alarm clock on the wall, which said that the time was 5:30 a.m. Tomas got dressed in the clothes that were at the end of his bed. After that he walked into the bathroom and brushed his teeth with a new toothbrush that said "Tomas" written on the side. He washed his face and combed his blond hair to the side.

When he turned around to leave the bathroom, he saw Nathan in the doorway. "I saw your future," Nathan said. "For your own safety, don't ever go looking for your father. If you do … just don't."

"Okay," Tomas said awkwardly. Then Tomas saw Roger's hand appear on Nathan's shoulder. Nathan was suddenly thrown out of the way and to land on the floor with a thud.

"Don't scare the kid with your creepy mind," Roger threatened.

Tomas was shocked that Roger would do that to Nathan. "Back off, Roger!" he yelled.

"Dude, this kid is trying to scare you with his demented mind," Roger said. Nathan looked up at Tomas from the floor and wiped his nose, in disbelief that someone was actually standing up for him.

Then Nathan glared at Roger and hissed, "Enjoy the last month of your life. You're no match for what's to come."

Tomas extended a hand down to Nathan and helped him up. Then Freddy hopped out of bed and said to Tomas, "Holy cow, man. Did you just stand up to Roger?"

"Yeah, why?" Tomas said back.

"Dude, he is the toughest guy on the ship," Freddy said.

Before Tomas could say something back, an alarm rang, and all the boys hopped out of bed and quickly got dressed. Tomas followed them out the door and along hallway until they got to a pair of doors. When they opened, Tomas smelled the sweet aroma of syrup and bacon. He figured that this was the cafeteria.

Tomas went and sat down at a table, expecting the food to be served to him, but that wasn't the way it worked at all. He looked at a line of boys and girls and saw them with their swords in their hands.

Patrick walked over to Tomas and said, "If you want breakfast—or any meal—you have to fight a hologram of a standard peacekeeper. Tomas was very confused about why they couldn't just hand the food out, but he followed Patrick to the line of people. When it was Patrick's turn, Tomas paid careful attention to how he fought the hologram. When it was Tomas's turn, he heard Patrick say, "If you don't win, you don't eat. It all ties in to training."

Tomas stepped into the small arena and saw a new hologram of a peacekeeper forming. When Tomas charged the peacekeeper after it was complete, he found out that the peacekeeper was a lot more skilled than the ones in the heating room. After five minutes of relentless fighting, every muscle in Tomas's tense body ached. He was about ready to give up. He dropped to his knees and said, "Okay, you win." The peacekeeper approached him and raised his sword over his head. And that was when Tomas had a brilliant idea. He took his sword and pushed it through the peacekeeper's chest, making the peacekeeper disappear.

"Come and get your breakfast," an older lady at the food counter said. Tomas walked over and saw pancakes with bacon and syrup. Then he took his brimming tray over to a table where Allen, Nathan, and Patrick were sitting.

"Hey," Tomas said when he sat down. They all looked at him with their mouths open. "What?" Tomas said after shoving a piece of bacon into his mouth.

"You made it," Nathan said. "When we fought the peacekeeper hologram for the first time, we only lasted for, like, ten seconds."

Then Allen added, "What we're trying to say is that none of us were fed for a week, or something like that."

Then Tomas added, "I'm just a normal kid … right?"

"I think you're more than normal," Patrick said seriously. "I think you're the one the Nova Guard has been looking for—the one who can end all of the evil in the galaxies."

"That's not me," Tomas said. "I was a normal kid who lived on a normal planet until I found some sword that changed everything for me."

Two girls came over to the table and sat down next to Tomas. "Tomas, I would like you to meet Valery Aster and Polly Bolt," Allen said. Valery had short, black hair and was about the same size as Tomas. Polly looked a few years younger than he was. She had curly blonde hair and was so pale that Tomas could have mistaken her for a ghost. Both girls gave Tomas a quick nod and then started talking to each other about the Capture the Flag training.

Tomas ate quietly, and after a while listening to their conversation, he suddenly blurted out, "Why don't we hide in trees above our flag, and when somebody comes to take the flag, we just tag them or something?"

"That could work!" Valery said.

"It actually could," Nathan added. "But since it's only the six of us, we're going to have to spread out."

"Wait, our table is our team?" Tomas asked.

"Yep," Polly said proudly.

"Okay, Tomas," Nathan said. "Finish up, and let's go place our flag somewhere. Well, I already know where we're going to hide it. And it's a good place."

Director Pierce came into the cafeteria shortly after everyone had left. He strolled straight over to Mrs. Fandom, the cafeteria worker, and said, "Did the boy pass?"

"He did, sir," she said. "He put up a long fight, and in the end, he faked a surrender. When the peacekeeper came over to make him lose, he hit him right in the stomach. I have to admit, I was impressed. Do you think he is … the one?"

The director paused. "Maybe he is, but I will find out if he truly is the one today in his first training session. Hail, Check."

CHAPTER 2
Spies and Pirates

Tomas, Patrick, Allen, Nathan, Valery, and Polly walked into a room along with all the other kids. The room was not very big, so Tomas started sweating quickly.

"Tomas, put your sword up onto that conveyer belt, and then walk over to a yellow flag," Polly whispered.

As Tomas walked toward the conveyer belt, he noticed a rainbow of colorful flags lined up, spread about ten feet apart from each other. The flags were like large handkerchiefs.

He put his sword down on the conveyer belt and noticed that Roger and a few other bulky kids walked over to a red flag, all smirking at the kids who weren't as strong as they were. Tomas felt anger boil up inside him when they started pointing and smirking at Nathan. He wanted to go over and punch Roger, but he knew it would only make Roger an enemy and not solve any problems.

Tomas walked over to a yellow flag and asked Patrick, "Can Allen use his power during the game—you know, where he makes thing float around him?"

"No," said Patrick. "If you do, you're disqualified. And that's not all. If someone is hurt when you use your power, then Director Pierce will usually abandon you on the closest planet."

"Has anyone ever done it before?" Tomas asked.

"Oh, yeah," said Patrick. "It's in a person's nature to retaliate if he's attacked. And if you happen to have a power, then the anger takes over your body, and you involuntarily release all your anger on them."

Suddenly, a voice started calling names. "Nathan Winter," someone yelled. Nathan walked up to a tall man, and Tomas saw that he handed Nathan his sword back. Tomas noticed that Nathan's sword now looked very different, for the custos's glass ball had been removed. Tomas soon knew why. It was so you would not know when someone was near. It was also probably because that was where all the power was—or at least that was what Pete had said. When Tomas got a glance at Nathan's sword, he also noticed that it looked like a regular sword, like the ones in books.

"Um, Nathan," Tomas asked, "do we win?"

"I don't know," Nathan answered. "I can only see certain things."

Tomas thought about this until he heard a man shout, "Tomas Knight."

Tomas squeezed his way through the crowd of kids until he reached the same tall man that Nathan had gone up to. The man handed him his sword and whispered, "Good luck." And then he called the next person up.

As Tomas headed back toward his flag, a hand grabbed his shoulder. It was too big to be that of a normal kid. Tomas didn't look back until he had been led into a smaller room. He heard the door close and then looked behind him. Director Pierce was standing in front of the door with his hands behind his back. "Tomas, it is good to see you again. Are you well?"

"Why have you brought me in here?" Tomas asked.

"Because of what you know—or think you know—about Peter Rack. Do you know what his background is? You see, Peter did not live on Frozer for thirty years. It's too cold to live there. And do you really think that Peter survived the Fleet 404 crash? Peter used to work for the Astro Army, but one day he found a sword, and it corrupted him. He wanted power, so he decided that if he could find a way to bring all of those dead peacekeepers back to life, he could accomplish anything. So after he raised an army of the dead, he tried to start a war that didn't need to be fought. But his army rebelled when the Nova Guard started picking them off one by one.

"So Peter hijacked the lead ship of Fleet 404, stole a Nova Guard vehicle, and pretended he was the scout ship. He radioed all the ships that he had gotten orders from me to land on Frozer. Well, once they entered the atmosphere, the ships were too heavy to slow down and create drag. The entire fleet crashed, but he lived. When he landed, he burned a Nova Guard base and left his ship in the only standing warehouse. Just thought

I'd let you know the man with whom you were 'friends.' That is all. You are dismissed."

Tomas could hear Pierce chuckle to himself, and he walked out of the room in complete shock. Had Pete really been the man Director Pierce had just described to him? But then he heard the director whisper to himself, "Children are so gullible." Tomas knew what Pierce was trying to do. He was trying to make Tomas distrust Pete if he ever came back, which he would.

As Tomas left the room, he noticed that all the flags and kids had left through an opening that led into the arena. Tomas, still a bit startled, cautiously walked toward the entrance to the arena. Once inside, Tomas felt the chilly air hit his skin. He saw that all the giant rectangles had somehow been replaced by massive wooden walls. They towered over the trees, casting massive shadows over the arena. At the end of the first wooden corridor stood his team, all cloaked in yellow jerseys. Allen tossed Tomas a jersey when he drew close. Tomas put it on.

Valery asked, "What did Pierce want with you?"

"Oh, he just wanted to make sure I was doing okay," Tomas responded.

"You know, there have been some rumors going around that Pierce works for the Checks. I don't believe them. I mean, the guy could be doing much better things with his life than this, but he likes this place so much that he personally pays for all repairs on the ship. It costs like four hundred thousand units to fix something on this floating scrap yard."

Units were the system of money for the entire universe. But some places only accepted things with sentimental value in a kind of trade system.

"Guys, come look!" Patrick said excitedly. They all ran over to him and saw him sitting down, looking at the wooden wall. When Tomas got close enough to see what Patrick had found, he saw a small hole in the wall.

"This is a great place to hide our flag!" Allen said happily.

When Patrick reached out to put the flag into the small hole, he made a strange face. Tomas heard the sound of paper being crinkled. After a moment, Patrick took out a small piece of paper that had a map of the ship on it.

"What's that?" Allen asked, pointing to a small red line on the outside of the ship.

"It says 'Check Communication Center,'" Patrick said. "That means … that someone on this ship is working for the Checks."

"But if there's a communication center, that means there are more than just one person working for the Checks," Polly said excitedly.

"What does that mean for us?" Nathan asked firmly.

"Nothing good," Tomas said. "I think they might be trying to turn us into weapons for the Checks."

"Then let's get to the bottom of it before it does happen," Valery said.

"But sometimes running away from a problem is necessary," Nathan said slowly.

Tomas watched Patrick put the piece of paper into his pants pocket. "We'll discuss it at lunch," he said.

"But first we should tell Director Pierce," Allen said.

"Good idea," Nathan said. "But let's focus on the game for now."

Once their flag was in the hole, which was a much better hiding spot than the tree they'd originally planned to hide it in, they decided to split up into pairs and go in different directions to try to capture the other teams' flags.

Tomas was with Allen. They decided to leave the wooden maze and head to the part of the arena with the trees and bushes. When they got there, they quickly noticed an orange flag sitting in the bushes. The surprising thing was that no one was protecting it. "Um, okay. That's random," Tomas said.

"Tomas, if you hit someone, that person is going to dissolve," Allen said. "But don't be frightened. If you get hit, then you appear back in your dorm on the metal pad you saw when you first came here." He and Tomas approached the flag.

When Tomas was only about ten feet away, he caught a glimpse of something orange in a bush about five feet away. He whispered, "Wait! It's a trap. They're waiting in the bushes."

"Oh, please. Someone would have shown himself by—"

"Watch out!" Tomas screamed as he saw someone lunge from the bushes at Allen.

Allen screamed as he turned to see two people in orange run toward him. He tried to back up but tripped over his own feet and landed on the ground. Two people in orange jerseys jabbed him with their swords at the same time. Tomas watched in shock as Allen slowly dissolved. When his legs were completely gone, he said, gasping for air, "Grab the flag." And then he vanished completely. Then more people in orange appeared from the bushes and charged at him.

Tomas had only one idea: to run. He ran back toward the wooden maze, and when he looked behind him, he noticed that all but one person were running after him. He ran straight into the maze to where his team's flag was before stopping to take a breath. As he was resting, he had an idea.

Tomas walked behind a corner and heard the yells of the others in orange getting louder. He hoped that when they turned the corner he could hit them, one at a time, until he could go back and get their flag. When the first person turned the corner, Tomas struck him across the chest. He did this to everyone who came through—until the two people who had hit Allen came through. Time seemed to freeze when Tomas saw who they were. But it was too late to stop his swing, and now they were starting to dissolve. They were Freddy and Teddy, his roommates. Once they had both completely dissolved, Tomas ran back into the maze.

About ten minutes later, after he'd captured three other flags, Tomas heard a voice from a speaker somewhere in the arena, saying, "Yellow wins. Yellow wins." As the walls started going back down, he was completely dissolved.

When he appeared back in his dorm, Tomas heard Allen, Patrick, and Nathan bellowing, "Yellow won! Yellow won!" Tomas took a look around and noticed that everyone who wasn't on his team was staring at him, openmouthed in amazement that he had won the game for his team after being at the academy for only one day.

As Tomas was pulled off the metal pad by his teammates, he said with a smirk to everyone else, "You know, it's rude to stare."

Questions were swirling in Tomas's head. "How did I win the game?" he asked.

Allen explained. "When you were running through the maze, Patrick went to get the orange team's flag, because their flag was the sixth one left. Just as he touched it, a guy in purple hit him. When you touch someone else's flag, everyone on that team disintegrates."

"That was a really short round," Tomas said.

"Yeah, I think that was the shortest round ever," Nathan added. "Maybe like thirty minutes."

Tomas noticed that in the twelve hours he had known him, Nathan's mood had changed a lot—from creepy and gloomy to bright and happy.

Suddenly Roger said, "Come on, guys, it's just beginner's luck. Get over it."

"Um, Roger, how many times have you won by a millisecond?" Patrick asked.

"Wait, what?" Tomas said.

"Oh, yeah," said Patrick. "Some girl on green took out Valery right as she touched their flag. That made *you* the winner." He smiled.

"I'm going to recreation," Roger muttered.

"What's recreation?" Tomas asked.

"It's where you get to chill and do fun activities while you wait for your next training class," Allen said. "Come on. Let's go."

After a minute's walk up a long hall and a flight of stairs, Nathan opened a door. Beyond the door were several elevators. Tomas read the sign above one of the elevator door. It said "Custos Retrieval." Tomas asked Allen if he should go and get his custos. Allen told him he could get it if he wanted to.

Tomas did want to. He walked over to an elevator packed with other people. When the doors closed, Tomas heard a Nova Guard soldier in back of him whispering to himself, "I'm sorry. I'm sorry. I'm sorry."

Tomas began to get suspicious. "Are you okay?" he asked the guard.

"Yeah. But… you're not," he replied.

At that moment Tomas saw him pull a gun out and saw one word on the side of it: "Check."

Tomas quickly spun around and lifted the man's gun arm into the air. Tomas fired the gun wildly at the small celling until it was out of ammo. All the other kids in the elevator either ducked down and put their hands over their heads, or helped Tomas by kicking the man or punching him. The man let out a sharp cry of pain and fell to the ground, crumpled into a ball.

"Who else is working for the Checks on this ship?" Tomas demanded.

"I'd rather die than tell you."

"Tell me!" Tomas screamed.

"Okay, okay," the man whimpered. "Almost every soldier on this ship is working for the Checks. General Ventex is trying to turn you into weapons for his army. He—" A loud boom interrupted the man. "We're under attack," he whispered.

Tomas wondered who could be attacking them. The Nova Guard thought that this ship he was on was a school. The Checks knew it was a ship full of spies. Then Tomas remembered the one group he hadn't considered: space pirates. Space pirates were ruthless people who would take over any ship they saw. They almost always traveled in groups of hundreds, or maybe even thousands. For the most part, they lived on asteroids or colonized small towns on dwarf planets like Makemake, Pluto, or Eris. Tomas heard another boom followed by the sound of engines stopping.

"They hit us in the engine room," the soldier said.

"How do you know?" Tomas said.

"Because they've attacked us before," the soldier said.

When the elevator doors opened, Tomas said to the soldier, "Don't even think about moving. We've got swords, and you have an empty gun. Who do you think would win?"

Tomas ran over to a table full of custos balls. He scanned them all quickly and soon found his. He knew it was his because underneath the glass ball was a note that said, "Tomas Knight, fifteen years old." He quickly snatched it and put it back on the butt of his sword.

Suddenly, Director Pierce's voice came through a loudspeaker above them. "Attention, all students. For your own safety, please report to the dining hall immediately. Thank you."

The soldier then blurted out, "Well, you heard the man. Back in the elevator."

"How about you stay here?" Tomas said, walking up to the soldier and pointing his sword at him.

"Okay, okay. Just don't hurt me," he answered. He stepped out of the elevator and walked over to a corner and sat down with his hands in his face. "Please," the soldier said. "I don't want to die."

"You will probably be safer down here," Tomas said as the other kids entered the elevator. With that, the doors closed and they were off.

"Hey, Tomas, nice going back in Capture the Flag," said a voice from behind Tomas. He looked behind him to see Valery leaning up against one of the elevator walls with her arms crossed.

"Thanks," Tomas said, blushing at the compliment.

"You still think we should tell Pierce about you-know-what?" Valery asked. "And maybe about the soldiers being spies?"

"Definitely," Tomas replied. "Let's go straight to his office."

"Do you know where his office even is?" Valery asked.

"No, but I bet I could find it," Tomas said. When the elevator doors opened, Tomas saw students running out of an elevator, screaming. When Tomas and Valery walked over to see what was in the elevator, they both screamed and jumped back. There lay Patrick, his entire left sleeve soaked in blood.

Valery gasped. "What happened, Patrick?"

"The soldier … shot me. He was working for those bloody Checks. He pulled a gun … shot me …" And then Patrick passed out, probably from blood loss.

"Let's bring him to the infirmary," Valery commanded.

In the twelve hours that Tomas had been on this ship, he had seen enough for a lifetime. He picked Patrick up by the feet, and Valery picked him up by the arms. Tomas kept following Valery, who was looking backward as they moved along.

"How long have you been here?" Tomas asked her. "You seem to know these halls like the palm of your hand."

"I've never heard that saying," Valery said. "Oh, right. I've been here since I was eight. Don't even ask about my parents. They didn't care for me a bit. Not seen them for seven years." Valery backed into a door to open it, and Tomas saw beds lined up in a row.

"This boy needs help!" Tomas screamed.

Suddenly, several nurses came through a door at the end of the infirmary. They ran over and took Patrick from them. "You kids should get to the cafeteria," one of the nurses said.

Tomas and Valery quickly ran down a set of hallways and eventually got to the cafeteria doors. When Tomas opened them, the smell of bacon and syrup was gone. Now it smelled like sweat and nervous kids. They slowly made their way over to their table where Allen, Nathan, and Polly were sitting.

"Where's Patrick?" Allen asked.

"Remember that note about the Checks and how there are some on this ship?" Valery said. "Well, it was true. Two soldiers working for the Checks went in two different elevators, both armed with guns. Both wanted to end us. I don't know why. Patrick was in one of the elevators that were attacked. He lived, but the soldier shot him in the left arm. He's in the infirmary right now."

Everyone at the table except Tomas stared blankly at her. After a few moments of silence, Director Pierce walked into the room and onto a stage that Tomas hadn't noticed before.

"Crud. We forgot to go straight to Pierce's office to tell him," Valery said.

Director Pierce yelled, "Attention, children. As you know, the ship is under attack. But do not worry. Our soldiers are handling it well. Even though the space pirates have—"

"Space pirates!" kids started screaming. Tomas looked up into Allen's stern face.

"Tomas, I'm sure you've never heard of these thugs before," said Allen. "If they spot a ship they think might have valuable cargo, they tear it to pieces using these things called *killers*." Killers are circular saws that have a cockpit mounted in the middle of the saw." At that moment, Tomas heard screaming from behind him and saw kids running in every direction.

Only twenty feet or so behind Tomas was a space pirate.

The pirate was wearing a torn green leather jacket and black leather pants. On his head he had a helmet with a visor. Green goggles prevented Tomas from seeing the pirate's eyes. He had on green boots, and a bandana around his mouth, and Tomas spotted hints of blood on him. In his hands he held some kind of laser gun, which was also green. Tomas's first instinct was to run from the pirate, but something told him to stay and fight.

As he drew his sword from his belt, he heard Nathan yell, "Come on!" Tomas turned around and headed toward Nathan. As Director Pierce passed him in the hallway, he said, "Tomas, sometimes trying to be a hero can save people. But sometimes, when you think you're doing the right thing by fighting for yourself, you're putting others in danger."

"Okay, listen," Tomas said angrily. "Can you just stop scaring me with your stories? I mean, first you tell me that my friend is evil, and now you're telling me that if I try to help you when you need me most, then someone will end up getting killed or hurt. And did you know that this ship is full of spies for the Check Army?"

"Really?" Director Pierce said, surprised. "Well, once the space pirates have been captured, I will have a talk with you, and anyone else, about what is happening. Good day."

With that, he turned down another hall that had soldiers running all along it.

"Tomas," someone said, clearly agitated. "Come on."

Tomas saw who it was. There was Nathan, ready to run down the hall. "Do you want to go back to the dorm and live another day, or stay out here and live another hour?" he asked.

Tomas ran up to Nathan, and they both started running down a hall. "Our dorm," Nathan said, "had to be the one closest to the battle."

"Where's Patrick?" Teddy said as they entered their room. Nathan just gave him a look, and Teddy suddenly became quiet and looked down.

Roger walked over to him and said, "Hey, how about you be a meat shield for us? I mean, you look like the kind who could take multiple shots to the stomach and only cry a little." Roger smirked and continued. "But really, if the space pirates do make it this far, then we are going to lock you out in the hall so we can escape."

"Shut it, Roger," Allen said.

After half an hour of lying in bed and praying that he would live, Tomas saw a black-and-red object go whizzing by the dorm window. Tomas remembered that the Nova Guard uniform was red and black, and he knew that the pirates were near. Everyone but Tomas ran over to the window and screamed, "Peacekeepers and pirates are coming!"

Then they opened the door, and all of them ran out—except for Roger, who had been trampled as they were leaving. Roger started moaning while holding his ankle. Tomas knew that he couldn't leave Roger here, but couldn't carry him out either. Tomas knew it was time to be the hero that Director Pierce didn't want him to be.

"Hello, Director Pierce," General Ventex said as he walked into the director's office.

"What do you want?" Director Pierce said angrily.

"I've come for the boy," General Ventex said. "Mrs. Fandom, the lunch lady, contacted me. She said the boy showed unbelievable strength in your training session before a meal. Did he not?"

"So you attacked my ship!" Director Pierce shouted. "You made an alliance with space pirates! You decided to harm the children you can use as weapons one day—instead of just asking me to give the boy to you! You even told two of your soldiers to attack children in elevators—just to create a distraction!"

General Ventex said, "I gave you plenty of time to turn kids who are special into weapons for the Check Army. You see, Director Pierce, you are the reason for many Check battle failures, and I will not tolerate that. Guards!" Suddenly, two tall guards walked into the room, equipped with rifles that had bayonets on the front.

"You called, sir," said one of the guards in a deep voice.

"Yes. Take this man away," General Ventex ordered.

"But … yes, sir," the guard said sadly. The two men escorted Director Pierce from his office and down a hall.

Tomas drew his sword from his belt and dragged Roger into the bathroom. "Roger, lock the door," Tomas whispered, knowing that anyone who tried to open it would not be able to do so. But Tomas also knew that the door would most likely be broken down.

As soon as Tomas turned around, he heard insane banging, and then the door smashed open. He looked at the wooden splinters on the ground and then looked up. Standing about ten feet in front of him was a man who looked just like the one he had seen in the cafeteria. The only difference was that his sleeves had been torn off to reveal his muscles.

The man stared at him and said, "You want to die."

He had a heavy accent, but Tomas didn't know what kind. "No, please," Tomas said with a grin.

"Think you so funny, ah?" the man said. "I don't like funny people."

"Okay," Tomas said.

The pirate charged Tomas, yelling and screaming.

Tomas grabbed his sword from his belt.

The man took out a knife and tossed his gun on the floor.

"Really?" Tomas said. "You would rather use a knife than a gun? Wow. That's embarrassing." He shook his head.

"What wrong with you? The knife—" The man pointed to his knife. "I throw."

"What if you miss me?" Tomas said. "Then what?" He tried to look serious, but inside he was laughing hysterically.

"I punch you. Sword does nothing."

"It can make me jump," Tomas said.

"What?" the man said.

Before he could figure out what Tomas meant, Tomas jumped over him. But before Tomas had made it completely over the pirate, he hit his head on the ceiling. He fell onto the man's head.

"Ow!" they both said simultaneously. After hitting the man's hard head, Tomas had another fall to the floor. Before he could get up, he felt himself getting lifted up by his shirt and pants.

That was when Tomas remembered the grappling hook. He pulled it out of his pants pocket and aimed it at the pole above the broken door. He pulled the trigger, and the hook went flying over to the metal pole and landed successfully. Tomas then went whizzing across the room. *Wow*, he thought. *They sell these at toy stores?* He had not expected to continue on through the doorway and go smashing through another door to bump into a peacekeeper who was leaning over a boy.

The peacekeeper fell onto the boy. Tomas quickly took the boy's sword, which lay in back of him. He slashed the peacekeeper's back, turning the man to dust.

"Mind if I borrow this?" Tomas asked the boy, who was now standing and wiping dust from himself.

"Sure. Take it," the boy stammered.

Tomas turned around and caught a glimpse of the pirate extending his arm toward him. He ducked, knowing a knife was coming. But when he looked behind him a second later, he saw the boy on the floor, the knife lodged in the his shoulder. Tomas suspected that the boy was about ten. He then realized that the boy would have been saved if Tomas hadn't ducked.

Even though the knife had hit the boy in the shoulder, he could still be in danger, because he would not be able to defend himself anymore.

Tomas slowly turned back to the man who had thrown it. "You don't know what you have just started. I was thinking of letting you live, but now you leave me no choice but to end you. I'm sorry that you were never taught right from wrong, but I think you should have learned that over the years. I hope you burn."

"And what you going to do about it?" the man asked. "You going to hit me with glowing needle? Huh?"

Tomas charged the man—and then thought of an alternative solution. He would try to pull off the same move the peacekeeper had done to Pete. He pointed his sword at the man, and a beam of light hit his legs and sent him back into the wall.

Tomas looked behind him and saw the boy gritting his teeth. He seemed about to pass out, just as Patrick had done, so Tomas dragged him across the hall and into his dorm room.

The pirate lay on the metal transport pad used for Capture the Flag. His head was bent down between his legs, and his stomach was smoking. Tomas started to feel bad about what he'd done. His father had told him to never kill a man unless he had harmed someone else.

Tomas pushed the boy under Allen's bed to keep him safe. Then he looked back at the doorway—and his heart sank. He had thought that the worst was behind him, but clearly he was wrong. He saw at least five pirates, two peacekeepers, a Check soldier, and someone else. Tomas quickly noticed who it was. Standing in the front of the group was General Ventex.

General Ventex was not very tall. He had short black hair with giant black sideburns running all the way down to his chin bone. He was wearing a black suit with a black bulletproof vest. In his hands he had a black sword—a saber of sorts. In his other hand was some kind of crystal. He pointed it toward the man on the floor, who was now giving off black smoke. Suddenly, the man vanished into the crystal. The general carelessly threw it behind himself, and Tomas watched as the peacekeepers swarmed to it and brutally fought for it.

"Hello, boy. You remember me, don't you?" he said.

"When Pete told me that you have a golden sword that is more powerful than every sword ever made, was he right?" Tomas asked nervously.

General Ventex softly said, "He was."

Tomas was now more afraid than ever. He watched as General Ventex took out a sword handle. It was pure gold with dashes of silver scattered through it. He took a custos ball out of his pocket and placed it on the butt of the sword where it belonged. Tomas saw that the custos was golden too. After Tomas heard the custos ball click in place, he saw General Ventex press a button on the side of the handle. Suddenly, a golden sword popped out of the top of the handle. Tomas did not notice any words on the side of the blade.

"It is such a nice sword, you must admit," General Ventex said. "It's such a shame that you will die because of it."

At that moment Tomas noticed the general's other sword come hurtling toward his chest.

Tomas jumped into the air, did a spin, hit the sword with his own sword, and watched as it went flying into a peacekeeper. The peacekeeper dissolved, as normal. Tomas landed perfectly on his feet, only a foot or so in front of the general. Tomas was proud at first, but then he saw that everyone in front of him except the peacekeeper was staring at him blankly.

"He's the one," one of the pirates whispered.

"Kill him!" General Ventex screamed. The Check soldier and the peacekeeper charged. The Check soldier was very small, so Tomas kicked him, and he retreated. The peacekeeper put up a fight, though. His sword turned things to ice. Tomas had to dodge a lot of that until he came up with a solution. When the peacekeeper fired his next ice beam, Tomas held out the sword given to him by the boy only about ten minutes earlier. He watched as the sword turned to ice. Once it did, Tomas smashed the ice sword on the peacekeeper's head, turning him to dust.

Tomas looked up at the pirates.

"Why aren't you attacking him?" General Ventex screamed.

"Sir, we can't," one of the pirates said reluctantly.

"Why?"

"Because of the prophecy of Dondo, sir," said one of the pirates. "It states that one day a young man will come and stop a rising evil with three companions."

"Well, do you see any other people here?" the general yelled. "Do you?"

"I do," said one of the pirates softly.

"What?" General Ventex turned around to face Tomas, who turned around to see what the pirate was talking about. He gasped when he saw Roger standing there with his sword gripped tightly in his hands.

Roger walked toward Tomas and whispered, "Thanks for the save."

Tomas watched as Roger picked up speed as he walked toward General Ventex and the pirates. General Ventex started running toward Roger, but suddenly he fell on his chest. He lifted himself onto his hands and knees and looked up at Roger.

"So, you think you can win without a fight?" General Ventex said.

"I'd prefer a fight," Roger said angrily. "You took away my family right in front of me, and you laughed when your men started beating them. You took them back to your ship, and you left me, all alone in my village—which you torched before you left. You also took all the supplies from my village and loaded them onto your ship, leaving me with nothing but charred wood from the houses."

Tomas couldn't believe what everyone's situation had been before the Nova Guard had taken them in. Allen didn't have any parents; Valery's parents didn't care that she existed; and Roger's parents had been taken from him by the Checks. It was all so terrible.

"Well, then, boy, if you want to end me, why dont just do it?" General Ventex said, raising an eyebrow.

Tomas could tell that Roger didn't think twice about the general's question. Roger raised his sword above his head and brought it down. As it was about to hit the general's head, Tomas saw a golden outline appear around the general's body. When Roger's sword hit the general, Roger went flying back through the bathroom door, which was half closed. Tomas heard moaning from inside the bathroom, which meant that Roger was still alive.

"Farewell, boy," General Ventex said to Tomas. "I've decided to wait to kill you. I'll do it in front of Pete or something like that." He stood up and gradually walked out of the room with the pirates following. One of the pirates looked back at Tomas through the doorway. Even though he didn't say anything, Tomas could tell that the pirate was saying good-bye.

"Wow, there's a prophecy about me," Tomas said to himself.

He went to check on the boy under Allen's bed, who was somehow awake. "Hey, did you win?" the boy asked.

"Sort of. Let's just leave it at that."

An unfamiliar voice that wasn't Director Pierce's came over the loudspeaker in Tomas's room to say that the attack was over. Tomas felt more relieved than ever. He helped Roger and the boy with the knife wound down the dented hallway and into the infirmary. He knew where it was this time, because so many people were walking down there with torn shirts or cuts on their faces.

When Tomas entered the room, he handed the two boys over to a nurse, who put them into rolling beds and walked them off. Tomas walked around looking for another nurse to ask if Patrick was all right. When he found one, his smile turned into a frown at the news.

"He's undergoing surgery right now," the nurse said. "His arm is infected with some kind of poison from the bullets."

"*Bullets*?" Tomas said, surprised. "I thought he was only shot once."

"No, no," the nurse said. "He was shot multiple times. Luckily, the bullets were all in the same general area of his arm place. Unfortunately, we can't save the arm. We have to amputate it or the poison will spread throughout his body and kill him."

Tomas walked off sadly to the cafeteria where many other boys and girls were gathered. They were discussing what had just happened. Tomas walked over to the lunch lady and asked for a snack. She pointed to the small arena, and Tomas said, "Never mind." He walked off and returned to his dorm to find Allen and Freddy standing in the doorway with their mouths wide open, staring at the mess. "The toilet," Freddy whispered, pointing to the smashed toilet that had water slowly coming out of it. Allen slowly turned to Tomas and said, "Did you do all of this by fighting?"

"Yeah," Tomas said, looking down at his feet. "Roger's in the infirmary along with some other kid who looked like he was ten."

"Robby?" Freddy said instantly. "Kid can't bleed himself out. It's his power. Not the best one, if you ask me."

Tomas now understood why the boy hadn't passed out when he started losing blood.

"He's just afraid of *seeing* blood," said Freddy. "That's when he usually passes out."

"Do you guys know where Director Pierce went?" Allen asked.

Tomas and Freddy both answered, "No, not a clue."

The two guards took Director Pierce to General Ventex's flagship, *The Argovince*. They threw him into a cell in the five-acre engine room.

A short time later, General Ventex came to visit him. "I have decided that I will be nice and let you redeem yourself as a high-ranking official in the Check Army. I have spared the boy's life. I will set you free and let you back into the army if you can find him … and end him. Now, go back to your so-called ship—and remember, you have one week. If you fail me again, I will have your head on my desk. Wait, that's messy. I will have you tossed out into space. That sounds fair and enjoyable." Ventex chuckled to himself.

Director Pierce frowned when he heard what would happen if he failed. He answered back, "Your faith will be rewarded, General."

CHAPTER 3
An Escape Goes Wrong

Right after the attack by the space pirates, Tomas and everyone else were given lunch without having to fight the hologram. It was cheese sandwiches and mashed potatoes. They all sat on the floor, because most of the tables were smashed or burned. Everyone sat in small groups, talking about the condition of the dorms or who had gotten hurt. Tomas sat with Allen, Nathan, and Valery.

"Where's Polly?" Tomas asked Valery.

"She got knocked into the wall pretty hard by a space pirate," Valery replied. "They say she has two broken ribs and a torn rotator cuff."

While still chewing a part of his sandwich, Nathan asked, "Why did you stay behind, Tomas? You should have come to the library with the rest of us. Only one peacekeeper showed up and was taken down in seconds."

"I stayed behind because you all trampled Roger on the way out the door," Tomas said angrily. He ate the rest of his lunch in silence.

Suddenly, a man went up onto the stage at the back of the lunchroom. He had a white helmet on his head and looked to be about twenty-five. He placed a microphone stand in front of himself and bent over to adjust it to his height. He tapped the microphone twice and then said, "Attention, students. I'm your captain, Captain Colton. I would like to inform you of a few things. First, we will be landing on Moon 562. If any of you have no clue as to what I'm talking about, I'm saying that we will be landing at one of Earth's moon colonies. We are going there to make repairs on the ship. You will be staying there for about a month. Second, you will all be sleeping in here tonight. Why? Because we know that more pirates and peacekeepers are still on the ship. Any rumors you have heard about Check spies on this ship are false. The elevator incident was just two drunken Nova Guard soldiers. They are in our jail at the moment for harming Patrick Doric. Thank you."

Tomas remembered Pete saying not to stay on the moon for too long. He'd said it was full of murderers and thieves.

That night, everyone received a sleeping bag. Tomas did not get any sleep, because everybody was talking and singing. He wished he could be back on his home planet, Hera, sleeping on a mattress with springs and a feather pillow. He wished he could see his dog, Henry, again. Most of all, he wished he could be sitting in front of a fire with his dad, discussing what had happened during the day. Tomas missed his old life, but he knew that life was behind him and that a new life lay ahead of him.

When Tomas heard a bell-like sound at about five, he guessed that it was time to get up. A few other kids sat up from their sleeping bags and looked around. Tomas looked back to where the lunch lady usually was and saw her coming out of a door and up to her normal spot.

Tomas sat in his sleeping bag for a few more minutes and just thought about the captain's announcement that any rumors about Check spies were false. Tomas knew that couldn't be. After all, during capture the flag his team had found a note saying that there was a Check control center, or some such thing, on the ship. Tomas looked over at Allen, who had been sleeping across from him, and saw that he was squinting his eyes and wiping away what his dad called "night sand" from his eyes. Allen stretched and yawned, and before he was completely awake, a booming voice from the loudspeaker came on.

"Attention, all students. This is your captain, Captain Colton. I'd like to inform you that all your classes have been canceled for today because some pirates and peacekeepers are still hiding on the ship. You will later be informed about where you are allowed to go on the ship. Also, Director Pierce went missing for about an hour the other day, but he is now back on the ship. Thank you."

After the loudspeaker had turned off, Tomas looked over at one of the monitors who was a Nova Guard soldier. He saw that the soldier stood there, stunned, with his mouth barely open. Tomas looked around and saw some other monitors exchanging worried looks. What could this be about? Had they found out that a hostile army was still on the ship? Tomas didn't know.

He asked Nathan if he knew what they were looking worried about. Nathan placed both his index fingers on his temples and closed his eyes. He remained like this for several minutes. Just as Tomas was about to walk off and go to the infirmary to see if Patrick and Roger were awake, he saw out of the corner of his eye that Nathan's eyes had opened—and were purple. "Um, Nathan, your eyes are purple," Tomas said.

Nathan then said, "I'm not sure if this is true or not—my readings are a bit fuzzy—but Director Pierce plans to kill you when we land on the moon. That's in one day. Tomas, you have to leave the ship this instant." Tomas looked to Allen and Valery to see what their suggestions would be. Allen looked like he was about to say something, but he looked away before he did. Valery just nodded.

Tomas stood up and said, "How do I leave this ship while in space?"

Nathan and Allen said their good-byes sadly. Valery snuck Tomas out of the cafeteria and led him down many halls. They passed the infirmary, and Tomas glanced quickly through the small window on the door to see Patrick rotating his left arm in circles. Something didn't seem right about his arm, though. It seemed to be a different color—silver, maybe? When they passed the ship's jail—or, as Tomas had heard someone call it, the brig—he got a quick glance through the open doors and saw Director Pierce scolding two soldiers in their cells.

Tomas grabbed Valery's gray hood and yanked it back.

"Hey!" Valery said.

"Hold on," Tomas said. He went into the jail room, walked right up to Director Pierce, and said, "Hail, Check." Tomas did this to see the director's reaction. Director Pierce turned around and looked at Tomas with a hard look.

"Boy, are you working for the Checks?" Director Pierce said.

"Yes, sir," Tomas said strongly.

"Then you deserve to be in here to be executed. I will have two—I mean three—men end you." And before Tomas could pull back, he was already locked up in a cell. Director Pierce then turned to Valery and said, "And as for you, young lady, I think you can spend some time with your friend." Valery started to run as fast as she could, but when it looked like she would be caught, she gave up. She closed her eyes and looked down. When she opened them again, she and Tomas were both leaning against iron bars.

"What was that?" she demanded, leaning toward Tomas.

"I'm sorry. I just thought that because Nathan said Director Pierce was working for the Checks, he would—"

"Did you think he would give you a medal or something?" Valery put her hands into her face. "Sorry. I'm sorry. I was being harsh. Let's just get out of this jail the old-fashioned way, and steal the keys with our swords."

Tomas remembered once seeing a movie where someone in jail stole the guard's keys with a piece of straw while he was sleeping. "It could work, but don't they have a guard here at night or something?"

"I can take care of that," Valery said.

"What—" But before Tomas could finish his sentence, he saw Valery snap her fingers, and Tomas instantly fell asleep.

"Sorry, Tomas, but I cannot afford any mistakes," Valery said to herself. Her personal power allowed her to snap her fingers in someone's face and cause him to instantly fall asleep for about an hour. She looked down at her hands, which were light blue now. She would have to save her energy for later. Oddly enough, most people could use their powers whenever they wanted for as long as they wanted—but not Valery. The color of her hands was her warning. When she snapped once or twice, they started turning blue. Once they turned purple, she herself would fall asleep.

After putting Tomas into a resting position, she walked over to the bars and asked the guard to come over to her. He did so, and when he got close enough, Valery snapped her fingers. The man fell to the floor, shut his eyes, and began to snore. Valery's plan was going as expected—until someone in a black robe and hood showed up with a sword. As the figure started walking toward Valery's cell, she saw two more like him following the leader.

Valery recognized the outfit soon enough. Three peacekeepers were walking toward her, one holding the keys to the cell. Valery wanted to run to the back of the cell and hide, but she couldn't. She was petrified with fear. The peacekeeper with the keys started running toward the cell to open it. While it was running, Valery saw a pair of two bone legs, almost as if a skeleton was under the cloak. It stopped right in front of the cell door and put the correct key in the lock. The door swung open, knocking Valery off her feet.

The peacekeeper stepped into the cell, grabbed Valery by her hood, and walked her out of the cell. It handed her over to the one who seemed like the leader, and then it walked over to the cell with the two whimpering soldiers in it. The peacekeeper put the key into the lock, and again the door swung open on the first try. It walked into the cell along with another peacekeeper.

Valery glared into the cell before the two black cloaks blocked her view. All she could hear were the snoring guard and the two whimpering soldiers, but all were silent after about ten seconds. Valery, now awaiting her fate, looked over at Tomas and snapped twice to instantly wake him. Valery looked down at her hands and saw that they were purple. As she fell asleep, Tomas woke up.

Tomas looked around and gasped. He saw Valery lying motionless on the floor with three peacekeepers staring at her. Tomas looked over at the two soldiers who were in the elevators and saw that they too were motionless. Tomas stood up and drew his sword from his belt. He started walking toward the peacekeepers, still unnoticed. When he was about a yard away, one of the peacekeepers turned around, but before it had made sense of what was happening, it was dust—along with the other one.

The last one turned around quickly enough to block Tomas's sword blow. It fought Tomas for at least an hour, when Tomas finally hit the peacekeeper on the hand. It let out a grunting noise and then darted out of the room and down the hall. After a minute or two of panting as he leaned against the iron wall, Tomas heard a little squeak come from Valery. She suddenly jerked upright and looked around frantically. When she noticed Tomas, she let out a sigh of relief. "Still want to leave?" Valery asked.

"After that? Of course," Tomas said. "But I think I'll need some company."

Valery went to the cafeteria and found Nathan and Allen playing a card game. "Who wants to go on a little trip with Tomas?" Valery asked excitedly.

Tomas went into the infirmary and found Roger with a bandage on his arm, reading a magazine. "What was that foot thing about?" Tomas asked with a smile. "Did you fake that because you knew General Ventex was coming?"

"Yeah," said Roger with a smile.

"Want to go and create our own story?" Tomas said.

"As long as I don't let the Nova Guard write it for me," Roger said.

"That could be arranged," Tomas said happily.

"What are you guys talking about?" came a voice from behind Tomas. Tomas turned around and saw Patrick. His left arm was … metal. Patrick had a robotic arm. The gears and other parts had been covered with metal, making it look like he had dipped his arm into silver paint. "They had to cut off my own arm because it became infected," he said.

"Hey, Patrick, wanna come on an adventure?" Tomas said.

"Where?" Patrick asked.

"I dunno. Anywhere to get away from this place," Tomas said.

A smile appeared on Patrick's face.

Tomas met up with the others at the jail entrance, and Valery led them all down a long flight of stairs and into a room bustling with workers.

"Welcome to Bay 1," Valery said. "Stay here." She walked over to a red lever and pulled it. A sharp alarm came on, and all the workers froze for a second before running up the set of stairs Valery had just led them down.

"Fire alarm!" shouted some of the men. Once they had all evacuated the area, Tomas saw a large Nova Guard craft about the size of the one he'd seen in the bunker back on Frozer. Next to it was an even larger ship that was mounted with dozens of blasters. Then a man who looked a lot like Tomas came up to them.

"If you are going to escape, take that one," the man whispered, pointing to the larger ship. They all ran toward it. When Tomas looked back at the man, he was sprinting up the stairs.

Tomas smelled food from the outside of the ship, which meant that lots of food had to be inside. They all followed Valery up a platform and into the ship. "Roger, go press that blue button over there," Valery ordered, pointing toward a small blue button on the wall about twenty feet away from the ship. Roger ran and pressed it, and Tomas felt the floor moving. He ran up to the cockpit where Valery was sitting and looked out the cockpit window. He saw the floor of the room split into two sides, leaving an opening big enough for the ship to fit through. Tomas heard Roger run back onto the ship, and he saw Valery press a button that made the entrance platform close. Nathan and Allen joined Tomas to look out into the inky abyss of space. The ship was now in flight, and the Nova Guard academy was now just a dot in space.

About an hour after their escape, Valery asked Tomas to take control of the ship for a while. Tomas did as he was told, and he soon found out that flying the ship was a lot easier than he'd expected.

After a few minutes, Patrick visited Tomas. "Tomas, what should we do now that we know there's a Check control center on the academy?" he asked. "I mean, all of those kids' lives are in our hands, because we're the only ones who know about the Check spies aboard the ship."

"No, they'll figure it out soon enough," Tomas said.

Patrick sat down in the seat next to Tomas and said, "So, what should we call our new ship?"

"Hmm ... maybe ... the *Star Light*," Tomas offered proudly.

"Good name," Patrick said with a faint smile.

At that moment, Tomas started feeling the same cold sensation he'd felt in the Nova Guard craft with Pete. His bones started aching, and he felt light-headed. Then he fell asleep.

Patrick gave a sigh of frustration and grabbed Tomas's fleece by the back with his metal arm. His new arm was extremely strong, and he had no trouble carrying Tomas out of his seat and bringing him into the bunkroom where Valery was resting. It was a small room. There were ten small cots, all stacked on top of each other, with about two feet of head-space. There were two ladders going up the side of the wall, giving access to all of the cots. Patrick put Tomas on the cot above Valery's and left the room.

He met up with Nathan on a bench against a wall, who sighed, "I guess he wants to go find his father."

"Then let him," Patrick said.

"No," Nathan said. "I saw his future, and I know what happens if he finds his father on this voyage. I'm saving his life, and I'm saving ours. Besides, we will have another opportunity to find his father later on, but I don't know if he will want to after that." They both sat on the bench in silence.

Meanwhile, Allen took control of the ship and kept it flying straight, until he saw something gray spinning in circles and bumping into other gray objects. To his left he saw Mars, and to his right he saw Jupiter. He soon knew what it was: an asteroid belt. And they were heading straight toward it.

"Guys!" Allen yelled. "Guys!"

Patrick, Roger, and Nathan all ran up to the cockpit. "Come on, turn around!" Roger yelled. Allen tried to move the joystick between his legs, but it was no use.

"It's jammed!" Allen yelled. "We're going to need some luck."

Valery had been wakened by all of the ruckus going on in the cockpit, and when she went to investigate, she saw the asteroid belt and knew what to do. She had a frantic look on her face as she went to wake Tomas up.

"Tomas, we can't have anyone sleeping right now," she whispered. "Put this on." She pointed to a dark-gray suit in a closet.

Tomas got out of the cot and walked over to the suit hanging in the closet. It was completely black and had built-in pads and some kind of hydraulics on the shoulder. He gradually put the suit on with a little help from Valery. He walked around the room while Valery went back into the closet and retrieved a helmet. The helmet looked strange. It was all black on the back half, but the front was covered with some kind of clear plastic that outlined the wearer's face.

Valery put the helmet on Tomas and twisted the neckpiece so it made a clicking noise. Tomas had lots of extra space where his face should be, but that was easily fixed when Valery pushed the plastic inward, right up against his face, giving him no room to move his head. Then she gave him gloves and a pair of boots.

"What exactly am I doing?" Tomas asked.

"You are going to take Patrick's custos and smash it," Valery said. "From there, Patrick will tell you what to say to the custos. Patrick can tell what custoses are saying, and he knows how to communicate with them. You will say what you hear Patrick saying. Patrick will tell you in the custos's language to destroy the asteroids, because the custos will become huge when not contained. It will make a path for us to pass through, and once we're out, I can find out how to fix the joystick."

Tomas just nodded, still not completely clear about what he was doing. Valery led him out of the bunkroom and across the hall through a door. Inside the room was a ladder, and that was it.

"Um, Val—" But before he could ask Valery what to do with the custos when he was done, the door had closed, leaving Tomas alone in the room. He walked over to the ladder and started climbing it. At the top of the ladder was a small hatch. He opened it by turning a knob, and above him lay the cosmic-latte color of the solar system. Tomas did not know why the color of the solar system was cosmic latte. Besides, a latte was an ancient drink, nearly two thousand years old.

As Tomas climbed up onto the roof of the craft, he made sure to keep a firm grip on something on the roof. He reached into his suit pocket and pulled out Patrick's custos. He said to himself, "I'm going to need some luck."

Tomas walked around on the roof of the ship to get used to his surroundings until he heard Patrick's voice come from his wrist. Tomas looked down and raised his arm close to his mask. He heard Patrick say, "Tomas, throw the custos ball down on the roof." Tomas did as he was told, still being a little bit hesitant. The glass smashed and was soon scattered off the ship and into space. Tomas took a few steps back, just to be safe.

The custos on the ground looked very light, and Tomas was surprised that it did not fly off. It started growing and growing until it was a massive, two-headed snake again. It was brown with black speckles on it. Tomas stood in wonder as he and his companions in the cockpit waited for the horrific screech of the custos. When the massive snake screeched, Tomas fell backward from the shock and lay on the cold metal roof. He started rolling off the roof but caught himself on an antenna.

Tomas held his arm up to his mask again and said, "Now what?"

"Say this to the custos: *Graaa jay foooom.*"

Tomas repeated the words he was told, and when he finished, the custos's heads both turned around and looked at him. It instantly shot its head back and slid right off the ship! Tomas gasped, but he was soon relieved to see that the custos was floating toward the asteroid belt. When it was close enough, Tomas saw it lunge its head forward, smash an asteroid, and come away looking completely unharmed. It stopped and waited for the ship, and when the ship got close enough, it looked forward and smashed a clean path right through the belt.

Tomas stood on the roof for about an hour, watching the custos make a straight path for the ship. He kept looking around him at the pieces of asteroid floating about, until he saw something lurking among the shadows of the asteroids. He didn't pay much attention to this at first, but then he saw it again and again.

Suddenly, a mass of pitch-black dragon-like things emerged from the asteroids and headed toward the ship. Tomas screamed and held his arm up to his mask. "Patrick! What are those?" he yelled.

"They're night mares," Patrick said in a normal voice. "They feed on fear. Stay calm."

"How am I supposed to stay calm when a thousand space birds are trying to kill me?" Tomas yelled.

"Hmm, good point," Patrick said.

Tomas figured that Patrick would be no help, and he lowered his arm. Then he remembered his sword, which Valery had randomly put on him when he was getting into the suit. He pulled it off the belt it was attached to and ran toward the swarm of night mares. He tried to act brave in front of the night mares, but inside he was scared for his life. When he slashed at the night mare closest to him, his sword cut it in half. Tomas now thought that this might not be so hard, but he was wrong.

As the dissected night mare floated away, Tomas saw out of the corner of his eye a strange mist emerge from its insides. He glanced over at the mist but now realized it was only inches in front of him. When he tried to back away from the black-and-purple cloud, he saw it lunge toward him and onto his mask. He fell asleep again, but this time it was because of the mist, not the cold. He had a feeling he might know what it was.

Tomas was suddenly in a dream. He saw himself in a grassy field, and only a few paces away were his dad and his dog. Tomas ran over to them and saw his dad kneeling down and extending his arms. His dog wagged its tail violently and kept looking around. When Tomas was only a foot in front of his remaining family, they vanished. The field suddenly turned black, and Tomas saw someone about one hundred feet away. He tried to move, but it was one of those dreams where you move really slowly. It aggravated Tomas a lot.

The person suddenly vanished and then appeared right in front of him. Tomas did not recognize the man. He had burns and scars all over his body, and what looked like frostbite on his nose. He also had a peg leg and a wooden crutch under one of his arms. He started laughing harder and harder. Then he screamed, "Ventex isn't the only one looking for Peter Rack! Ha, ha, ha!"

Suddenly, Tomas heard his name being yelled. He kept on listening until he forced himself awake. He jerked up and panted as he looked around him. He saw Valery and Allen standing nearby. Then he noticed he was lying on the strange-looking couch near the cockpit.

"Wha … what happened?" Tomas said, confused.

Valery answered, "We realized that you were being intoxicated by the night mare mist, because we heard thumping on the roof. Roger suited up and went up there and rescued you."

Tomas looked around for Roger but couldn't see him anywhere. "Where is Roger?" he asked.

"After he brought you down here, he had to go back up to retrieve the custos in this." Valery held up a golden cube. But he was also intoxicated, and, well, we had to send Nathan up to get him, but he too was intoxicated. Tomas, what I'm trying to say is … they're gone—but not dead, hopefully. The night mares carried them off to Saturn's hexagon. The night mares live there on the north pole of Saturn. We'd have a better chance of colonizing Titan than making it there. So, Tomas, since you are kind of our leader or something, I think you should make the call."

Patrick, who had been steering the ship while Valery fixed the joystick, looked back at Tomas with a smile. Tomas took a look around. If they went after Roger and Nathan, he might never get to see his father again. But if he went after his father, then his two friends might die. Tomas looked at the eager faces around him.

"I've come to a decision," Tomas announced. "Patrick, point this ship toward Saturn."

CHAPTER 4
The Rescue Mission

"Hello, Director Pierce," General Ventex said to the director through a telamonotor. "Have you done away with the boy yet?"

"Um … well, I gathered two peacekeepers, but—" Director Pierce tried to say.

"What happened, Pierce?" General Ventex said with an angry tone.

"He and some other students escaped on an H-29, sir. They pulled a fire alarm and—"

"I have heard enough, Director Pierce. I will be aboard your ship within the hour. I have decided to let you live … for now. You will be transported to Saturn's hexagon, which has the largest prison in the galaxy. Have you ever heard of Night Prison? It is patrolled by night mares—you know, those horrific black flying creatures. Yes. Good-bye, Director Pierce. I will see you shortly. By the way, my focus is not on the boy anymore. It is on finding Officer Hellmount. He is the other person who survived Fleet 404's crash—besides Peter Rack. He is badly burned and is rumored to have a peg leg, but he may still be helpful in my search for Peter Rack.

Patrick put the ship on autopilot for a while. Tomas and Allen had located the cargo hold and had found some food. They brought it up and set it on the table near the bunkroom. They all ate in silence until Tomas spoke. "Valery, can I ask how you knew all this stuff about the ship, and where everything was and all?"

"I usually spent my recreation time hanging out in Bay 1, because that's where everything was built," Valery said. "Sometimes I got to see some of the new Nova Guard models. For seven years I've been learning from the best how to control ships. And I learned how to fix things. The reason this one had a malfunction was because it was still being worked on. It may have a few more malfunctions before we arrive in the hexagon."

Valery's explanation wasn't as amazing as Tomas had thought it would be. He'd thought that maybe she had stolen ships and fought space pirates with them or something.

After dinner Valery found a pack of toothbrushes in the cargo hold, along with some toothpaste. After brushing, Tomas went and claimed the third bunk as his own. He didn't sleep well, knowing that two of his friends were probably having nightmares right now, more or less inside a night mare.

Tomas had heard the old sailors in his town tell tales about the hexagon, saying that it was the largest prison in the galaxy. They said that the air was bright red, and that if you escaped the hexagon, you would die from the gases of Saturn. Tomas shuddered at the thought of a night mare again. He remembered it being a fairly large black blob with no eyes, just a mouth with rows of teeth. He tried to erase the thought from his mind, but it was one of those thoughts that you couldn't escape. Eventually, Tomas fell asleep, but soon he remembered his duty, assigned by Valery. She had told him that he had to go take control of the ship about halfway through the night.

He hopped out of bed and moaned loudly. He didn't see why they couldn't just put the ship on autopilot and go to bed, but Valery said that someone always had to be alert in case of an attack. Tomas knew there would be no attack, but he did not want to fail Valery. He trudged toward the cockpit and saw Allen steering. The scene outside was a bit sketchy, but Tomas was not afraid. "Hey, Allen. You can go and sleep now. I've got this." He yawned as he waited for Allen to answer back, but he only heard little whimpers.

He walked up to Allen and saw that he wasn't even steering. His hands were on his face, and when he lifted his head, Tomas saw that his eyes were a bit red. "Have you been crying?" Tomas asked.

"No." Allen sniffled. "My eyes were sweating. Wait, that's gross. Yeah, I have. Tomas, if we go to the hexagon, you know there's a chance we might not come back."

"I know that, Allen," Tomas said. "But if we want to change things, like get rid of the Checks, we will have to take risks. We will take some losses, and we will get hurt, but it's all in the name of freedom—not only for us but for everyone the Checks have harmed. Think of yourself as a light in darkness. Wherever there is darkness, like among the Checks, there is light that will grow larger and larger until everything is illuminated—and the darkness is gone." Allen thought about this for a minute and then wiped his tears away and stood up.

"Well," Allen said, "if I have to die, I want to die alongside you, fighting for freedom. I've just realized that our small escape into nothingness could be the key to peace. We may just be kids, but age is just a number. Why can't we be stronger than the rest? Tomas, I'm no longer afraid of going to the hexagon, but I am afraid for Roger and Nathan. But, Tomas, we can't face the Checks alone, which is why I have contacted someone who can help us out. Tomas, I have contacted Peter Rack."

"All students to the dining hall, at once!" Captain Colton said over a loudspeaker. He hung up the microphone and sighed. "It's only a matter of time before they find out."

"Captain," someone said from behind him, "we have spotted a ship. We suspect it is *Argovince*. Why do you think it is coming, sir?"

Captain Colton turned around and looked at the man. "I'm tired of lying to the children, Mr. Gaffen. I think it's time they found out what they're really up against. That is why I have ordered them to the dining hall. I'm going to tell them the truth. But first, I need a visit with Director Pierce. The captain stood up and walked over to a closet door. He opened it and pushed the pile of Nova Guard suits out of the way to reveal a hidden hallway.

"Sir, I can't let you tell the children," Mr. Gaffen said darkly.

"And who's going to stop me?" Captain Colton asked. "You?"

Before Mr. Gaffen could shoot the captain, his own arm was throbbing from the captain's bullet. He fell to the ground and screamed in pain.

"As I said, who's going to stop me?" the captain said. He continued down the long hall illuminated with red lights. He entered the Check communication center—a large, dome-shaped, windowless room—and saw people scurrying around. The captain walked to the far end of the room where Director Pierce was sitting in a chair and looking at a screen. Captain Colton looked over his shoulder and saw that Director Pierce was watching a video about Night Prison.

"Sir, since *The Argovince* is coming and will subdue the ship shortly, I think we should tell the children the truth," the captain said firmly.

"Hmm. Well, I suppose," Director Pierce said.

That was easy, the captain thought to himself. He walked out of the room and down the hallway, but he was met by two Nova Guard soldiers—and by Mr. Gaffen, who acted as if he had never been shot.

"You really thought I wasn't prepared," Mr. Gaffen said, unbuttoning his jacket to reveal a bulletproof vest with iron alongside the arms.

The captain decided to take his chances and ran straight for the Nova Guard soldiers. They looked surprised, but instead of just standing there, they pulled their triggers and hit the captain in the chest a few times. The captain gagged and then dropped down at the feet of the soldiers. The soldiers and Mr. Gaffen walked around him and into the control room, meeting up with Director Pierce.

But the captain wasn't dead just yet. He pulled his body along the cold metal floor and up to the loudspeaker near the front. He leaned with one hand on the metal table, leaving the other arm dangling by his waist. He pressed the button and said with one final breath, "All of you students must escape while you still can. Look around you. Do you see those soldiers? They are working for the Checks—well, most of them are. Don't trust anyone, because you are all in grave danger. And if a man with burns and scars comes onto the ..." Before the captain could finish, he died.

After Allen went to bed, Tomas flew the ship for a bit. He discovered all kinds of cool buttons—like an antigravity one, and one that changed the color of the lights. He almost fell asleep a few times, but he resisted it. He heard yawns and footsteps and the sounds people make when they stretch. Tomas guessed it was morning, and he put the ship on autopilot. He saw

Patrick and Valery walk out of the bunkroom, and when he peeked in, he saw Allen, who was sound asleep.

Tomas ate breakfast quickly and went to lie down. Once he got cozy, he heard Valery and Patrick say simultaneously, "I can see the hexagon!" Tomas moaned and heard Allen wake up and hop out of bed, full of energy.

"Everyone, suit up. We will be landing soon," Patrick said happily.

"Wow," Tomas said. "The story of my life."

After suiting up in the same suit he had been in when he'd gone to the roof, Tomas tried to relax for a bit. He lay down on the couch and closed his eyes. This time he fell asleep and was not disturbed for another hour or so. He could have slept for a day, but he was awakened up by turbulence. He fell off the couch and onto the floor. He stood up and stretched, and when he looked forward into the cockpit, he saw mountains and tarnished air.

Tomas looked over at the only exit, which was slowly opening. Valery, who had a bulky blaster in her hand, soon greeted him. She handed the weapon to Tomas, and he saw that she had some kind of long, arrow-looking blaster.

When the ship landed, everyone ran out the opening with their blasters and their swords attached to belts of gadgets. Tomas added his grappling hook to his belt.

When the big platform went up again, they all stood in silence for a minute, until Patrick looked at the sky and yelled, "Someone's coming!"

Valery and Patrick ran and hid behind rocks, but Tomas and Allen stared with a smile. As the ship came into contact with the ground about twenty feet away, Valery and Patrick stood up from behind the rock and slowly walked over to Tomas and Allen. Tomas watched as the cockpit opened, and he soon recognized the craft. It was the Nova Guard craft that Tomas had traveled in a couple of days ago. From it emerged a figure that seemed to be carrying a blaster and a sword. He waved to the group and soon came into perfect view. Standing in front of Tomas and his friends was Pete.

"Hello, Tomas. I see that you couldn't stay out of trouble," Pete said with a smirk.

"Pete," Tomas said with a heavy heart.

"The night mares know we are here," Pete said. "Perhaps we should stay aboard your ship for a day or two, just so the night mares lose interest and think we are here for scientific reasons."

Tomas gave a quick glance over to Valery, who just nodded. They headed back toward the *Star Light* together.

After Tomas and Pete had talked about what happened in the past few days, Pete wanted to know who Tomas's friends were. Tomas identified each one. "That's Allen. He has a really cool power that may come in handy later on when we infiltrate the prison. That's Patrick. He has a metal arm because a Check soldier shot him a few days ago. And last, but certainly not least," Tomas said, giving a quick smile to Valery, "this is Valery. She can make people fall asleep whenever she wants just by snapping her figures. They all have swords. Well, not Patrick. His custos is floating around in space."

At that moment, Tomas and the others almost fell out of their seats when a startling knock impacted the end platform. They held their blasters at eye level, and Pete told them to stay there while he went and opened the door. As the platform lowered, Tomas heard a strange sound, but he soon recognized it. It was the sound of a scoot. When the platform landed on the dusty ground, a few Check soldiers were standing there.

"Hello," Pete said. "How may I assist you today, gentlemen?"

"Why are you here?" one of the soldiers asked.

"We have been sent by the Nova Guard for scientific purposes," Pete said.

"What purposes?" another soldier demanded.

"To collect rock samples to see if they have any water in them. If so, we might be able to start a scientific colony here."

"Hmm, and who are your helpers, may I ask?" a soldier said.

"They are children who were recruited from Earth because of their … um … skills in geological studies," Pete said.

"Hmm," a soldier said. "Then what is malachite?"

Tomas, who did know a fair amount about rocks and minerals, answered, "Malachite is a copper carbonate hydroxide mineral. It is green."

"Well, I guess I can allow you to continue your work. Good day. Also, don't go anywhere near the Night Prison, unless you want to have night mares," the soldier said.

At that moment, just when Tomas thought it was all over, the soldiers quickly turned around to face the group again. "Peter Rack, do you think we are that stupid? I mean, come on. Kids that know a lot about geology? I will make an exception for the boy who answered my question. And you're here to see if you can colonize a gas planet? No, it's all too good to be true. Now, drop your weapons and come with us."

Pete signaled for the kids to drop their blasters, which they did. Suddenly, only moments after he'd been disarmed, Pete took out his sword and waved it at the soldiers. "I'd scram if I were you, chaps," Pete said in a low voice. "Because if it comes down to the blood, we are a lot stronger than you."

Before anyone could react, Tomas saw all the soldiers collapse onto the ground.

"Huh?" Patrick said. Tomas looked at Pete and noticed that he was giving Valery a cold look. Tomas looked back at her and saw her face turning a bit red from the attention.

"Sorry, it's what I like to do," Valery said, looking down. When Tomas looked back at Pete, he noticed that he was smiling under his clear mask. Pete started laughing heartily. Tomas and Patrick gave fake laughs, but Allen thought it was hilarious.

"Come on, guys," Pete said. "Drag them into the ship. I'll put on one of their suits, hop on a scoot, and pretend you guys are prisoners." After Pete was all dressed up, he put the kids on the back of a scoot and headed toward the prison. Once again, everyone had a blaster and a sword tucked into their suits.

Tomas must have been on the back of the scoot for at least an hour before he heard Pete say, "Here we are." Tomas looked up and saw a massive red wall with red sand swirling around and over the wall. Pete started tapping on the wall, and it soon opened. "Got some prisoners for the warden," Pete said. "They'll make great slaves, they will. Nice and young, just how he likes 'em." The scoot slowly went into the courtyard as the big door closed again.

Tomas looked around and then whispered to Pete, "Who's the warden?"

"We used to work together until Fleet 404 crashed. I just found out yesterday from someone named Mr. Gaffen that he survived. I had contacted Gaffen to make sure everything was all right at the academy. He said that the warden of the Night Prison is a man named James Hellmount. He is said to have a peg leg and nasty scars and burns all over his body." Tomas's heart froze. Pete had described the man Tomas had seen in his nightmare. And the man had said he was coming for Pete.

Everything for the rescue mission was going as planned, so far. After making it out of the courtyard and into a massive room, Tomas started getting the feeling that he and the rest were being watched. The room was huge. It had massive black Corinthian columns near the wall that were stained with red sand. The red sand was scattered all around the room in small piles. Tomas noticed that Pete kept glancing nervously around the room, as if he had the same feeling Tomas did.

Once or twice, they could have sworn something was moving among the columns. As the scoot made its way onto a metal platform at the end of the hall, Tomas was jolted forward into Allen because the platform started rising up into the air. Tomas felt as if the scoot was floating. When the platform stopped at the top, Tomas saw that the scoot was headed down a red hall now, and he heard the platform go back down behind them.

"This is going great," Pete said honestly. Little did they know that someone waited only a few yards ahead, and it was not who Tomas would have expected.

The Argovince had easily taken over the academy, and General Ventex thought it would be a grand idea to take the children with him. Mr. Gaffen was in charge of rigging the ship with explosives so Director Pierce could see his life's work destroyed.

"What you're doing is wrong," Director Pierce said angrily as his hands were cuffed and was put back in his cell on *The Argovince*.

"No, it is not," said General Ventex. "It is a punishment for failing to capture the boy and turn everyone else into Check soldiers. I gave you thirty years." The general wore an evil smile, as if there was something he was not telling the director. "We will arrive at the hexagon in about ten minutes because of solar currents."

Director Pierce glared at the general through the bars. "You, General, are a terrible man."

"Oh, sure, call me what you want," the general said happily. "It doesn't affect me. The captain of your academy is dead, you know. Yes, killed only minutes ago … by Mr. Gaffen."

"No, Mr. Gaffen would never do such a thing," Director Pierce said. "He and the captain have been dear friends ever since they met."

"That was what you wanted to think. The entire time, it was an act. For five years Mr. Gaffen had to put up with your ignorant captain."

Director Pierce's heart sank. He stood silent, even after the general was gone. His only hope was a failed mission. He had counted on Tomas Knight to put an end to the general, and maybe to James Hellmount, but it wasn't likely. "Tomas," he said to himself, "you'd better still be alive. I'm sorry for my plots to kill you. It was all a … compliment. But I have not completely failed yet."

After making it about fifteen feet down the gloomy hall, Tomas and his companions could see someone waiting at the end of it. Other men soon joined the first, and they all seemed to be armed. They were most likely going to check out the "prisoners" Pete was delivering. As they drew closer, Tomas saw that the men looked like Check guards. They would tell Pete where the warden was.

But as he got a clear view, Tomas saw that one man was not a Check soldier but a man with a peg leg: Officer Hellmount. Pete quickly took out his blaster and fired at Officer Hellmount. He would have hit his target if the officer had not pulled out a golden sword and stopped the laser in midair. It floated there for a few seconds, and then the officer thrust his sword forward, making the laser change direction and hit Pete in the stomach.

Tomas closed his eyes, expecting the worst. For a minute, he heard the sound of wood getting closer and closer until he felt something take a firm grip around his neck. When Tomas opened his eyes, he saw that he was being held up against a column by a rough hand. He looked down and saw Officer Hellmount looking up at him. His gray eyes seemed to stare into Tomas's soul.

He said, "I know you're curious, boy. And I know you have always wondered about one question: what was there before time?"

Tomas had always thought about that question, and he would have loved to have it answered.

"Do you really want to know?" Officer Hellmount continued. "Before time, there was nothing but protons, and before that, there was darkness. It has mostly been destroyed over the years, but some still lurks in the shadows, hiding in space. This prison was not built by man but by the power that created the solar system: the darkness. It can take the form of anything it wants. It could even look like you. It took the form of a burned pirate many years ago. I am the darkness. I cannot die."

Tomas's heart froze. "I believe you can die," he said. "It's just that no one has ever succeeded in killing you." Then he saw the officer transform into his dad.

"Would you kill this?" the officer asked.

Tomas knew that this was not an officer. He was more of a shape-shifter. "I would if I had to," he said. "Depends what he was doing."

The officer then changed into Director Pierce, then into Pete, and then back to himself. Tomas felt the grip around his neck release, and he fell to the ground. "Silly boy," the officer said as he walked over to the scoot.

Tomas looked over at his companions, but he jumped back in surprise when he saw one of the guards who was holding Patrick go flying off of him and off the balcony-like hallway. Tomas heard the sound of metal, and knew the man had hit the platform. Tomas saw Valery snap her fingers, and the soldiers guarding her fell off like rag dolls. Patrick knocked both soldiers off the balcony with his metal arm. Allen just waited until his guards went to help the others, and then he hopped up and drew his sword and blaster and shot the rest of the soldiers down.

When Tomas turned around to face the officer, he was gone. "Come on," he said. "Let's go find Roger and Nathan." He was still a bit shaky from what had just happened. They put Pete's body behind one of the columns and left without the scoot. As they left the strange hallway, Tomas heard the sound of something hitting the building. Probably just a ship docking, he thought. But that ship was not just any ordinary ship.

Freddy and Teddy were in the same cell on *The Argovince* when the student captives were being escorted, cell by cell, into the prison. They screamed and cussed at the guards, who didn't seem to notice or care. When it was their cell's turn to leave the ship, they tried to punch the guards through the bars. They would have kept on doing this if a peacekeeper hadn't come up to them and pointed its black sword at their throats.

Polly didn't care that she was being sent to a prison where people died of hunger or thirst. She was more focused on her broken ribs, which still hurt, and her uncomfortable arm sling. She had a black eye from being smacked by someone named Mr. Gaffen for no apparent reason, and she was in lots of pain.

Director Pierce was the first to be escorted out of the ship and onto one of the landing docks. From there he was led into a large room with columns all over the place. He was led down many stairs and into what seemed like a boiler room, except for the fact that there was a small walkway in front of a cell, and lava spewing everywhere. Director Pierce soon knew where he was. About fifty feet below him was the pit of lava into which Officer Hellmount enjoyed throwing badly behaved prisoners. Director Pierce still had his sword on him, but when he tried striking the bars, he was electrocuted. His hand was still throbbing with pain from the battle with Tomas a day ago.

After a few minutes he heard the sound of a peg leg coming down the hall. He was greeted by Officer Hellmount, who informed him of Tomas's presence in the complex. He told the director that they would not make it far before they were caught and killed. After Officer Hellmount left, Director Pierce screamed and smashed his fist up against the bars. He needed to get his frustration out. Then he had an idea.

Tomas and his companions had made it through an empty dining hall, a cell room, and another random room with columns. They had finally gotten to a room that said "5-20," which Tomas guessed was the room for children. After he sneaked past some guards and a night mare, Tomas could see rows of cells filled with children. They were yelling and screaming and chanting, "The Nova Guard rules, the Check army drools! The Nova Guard rules, the Check army drools!"

Tomas scanned the cells, but he couldn't see Nathan or Roger anywhere. As he thought of turning back to explore more of the prison, he heard two voices—wait, *four* voices, all calling his name. Tomas looked over at a cell to his immediate left and saw Freddy and Teddy in the same cell as Roger and Nathan.

Tomas ran toward the cell with Valery and Allen and Patrick. Tomas shot one of his lasers from his sword at the lock and set the four free. They were all equipped with swords of their own. They all headed out of the room of children's cells and walked around the prison for a while, looking for Director Pierce to explain about the Check army.

After about an hour, Tomas saw the scoot they had arrived on, and he wanted to see if Pete was alive. When they got to where Pete should have been, they didn't find him. Instead they found a note.

Dear Tomas and friends,

I am in a lot of pain, but I am alive. I am off to a planet called Luminite. You do not need me anymore, because you are the masters of your own destinies, and you do not need another being as a guide down the river of life. There will be a few rocks in the river, and a few small waterfalls, but make sure you avoid those obstacles. If you aim to hit them, your boat will sink before it can reach the end of its journey. I thank you very much, for you have taught me that sometimes it is not good to avoid danger. Sometimes it builds up confidence, and that builds up courage, and that makes your boat stronger down the river of life. Remember, don't let your boat go down the wrong path. You are all sword bearers now. Sincerely, Peter Rack.

Tomas felt tears in his eyes. He didn't know why, but he now felt like he had the strength to battle an entire army of Check soldiers, and the courage and bravery to save someone from the most dire of situations. Tomas then had a feeling that he knew where to find Director Pierce. Even though he knew Director Pierce was working for the Check Army, he knew that under that weird old man was someone seeking adventure—or something. He knew that Director Pierce was a good man.

Tomas told everyone to follow him, and they did. He was now headed down at least one hundred stories of stairs. When Tomas took the first step on the stairway, he stopped, turned his head slightly, and said, "If anyone wants to stay back and not go down there, I suggest staying here. But if any of you want to come, then I need to know now." Tomas didn't look back to see who was coming, but he heard seven pairs of feet following him. He put on a bold smile and walked down the stairs.

CHAPTER 5
Falling into the Fire

For at least thirty minutes, Tomas and his companions descended the stairway. They were starting to get tired, but Tomas kept on walking downward. He was about ready to sit down for a while and rest, but soon he heard voices and yells from below him. His energy suddenly came back, and he ran down the remaining stairs with glee.

Once they were all at the bottom of the stairway, Tomas peered into the room from which he had heard voices. He looked in and saw a strange metal walkway only about four feet wide. To the left of the railing, cells were barely attached to the walkway, and they seemed to be floating over something orange-red in color. Colors glimmered on the metal, and the scene was quite amazing. On the right was nothing but bright colors. Tomas told the others to stay where they were, but he brought Allen with him because his power might come in handy if they ran into some guards.

Tomas slowly looked over the small railing and saw that the colors were actually boiling lava. He frowned at the sight. Soon he heard his name being called. He kept running toward the voice until it was right next to him. He looked over and saw who it was. It was Director Pierce.

"The children have found Director Pierce, sir," Mr. Gaffen said to Officer Hellmount. "We just saw them on a heat camera. What should we do?"

"I never thought this day would come. Mr. Gaffen, sound the evacuation alarm. This prison will not have anyone escape it. You and your men get out of the prison. Send General Ventex down there. I will be there shortly if they are not already gone. In one moment I will pull the alarm I thought I would never have to pull: the self-destruct alarm. This prison is going down in dust."

"Before I set you free and into our custody, tell me: why is everyone trying to kill me?" Tomas demanded of Director Pierce.

"Because you are the one prophesied by Dondo," said Director Pierce, "and General Ventex knows that you and your team are the only ones standing between him and complete power. He has recruited many people, such as Mr. Gaffen."

"Well, are you still going to kill me?" Tomas asked, crossing his arms.

"No, no. I am angry with the Check Army, and I wish to fight against them. Also, I am very sorry for lying to you about Mr. Rack. I know nothing about him except for—" Director Pierce was interrupted by the lock of his cell being blasted off. He stepped out of it and looked around nervously.

"So, what about Pete?" Tomas asked as Allen took a step back.

"Oh, yes, Mr. Rack is—why should I bother telling you? After all, you are my mission."

Tomas quickly sidestepped as Director Pierce lunged forward with his sword. Before Tomas could counter Director Pierce's next move, he was on the ground with a sword pointed at his neck. Patrick and the others ran to help Tomas, but suddenly a rumble came from above them and part of the ceiling collapsed. A few rocks fell right between Tomas and the others, breaking the metal walkway in half. There was a big gap between them now.

Tomas squirmed backward, but he felt his head drop a bit, and he knew that part of the walkway was gone. He could not take his eyes off Director Pierce's sword, which the director was slowly raising above his head. Tomas saw Director Pierce's hand shift a bit, and he knew the man was about to strike. He looked through Director Pierce's legs to look for Allen, but he saw that four Check soldiers had seized his friend. He knew that this was the end of his line.

Suddenly he heard someone behind the director say, "Stop." Director Pierce turned around and saw General Ventex emerge from the lot soldiers.

"Stop. Let me." The general looked down at Tomas's golden sword and gasped. "It can't be," he whispered. Tomas glanced at the general's sword and saw that it was glowing a deep blue. The general looked up at Director Pierce and said, "And you want to kill him for me." He lunged forward, tackling the director to the ground.

Tomas got up, scurried away, and pounced on the soldiers. Once they were taken care of, he helped Allen up. He looked back over at the scene and saw Nathan inching his way past the two. Nathan had jumped over the chasm because of one of his visions. "Tomas, we need to go!" Nathan yelled. "I saw something. The hexagon is about to shut down. Everyone here will die if we do not leave now. Tomas, come on!"

Tomas looked back at Allen to see what he suggested they do, but Allen was on the ground with his eyes closed. Tomas was relieved to see that he was breathing, but suddenly he saw Officer Hellmount appear next to Allen. Tomas didn't know where he had come from, and he didn't care.

Tomas ran forward to attack the officer, and then he noticed small, black blobs appearing on his body and starting to grow. He took his eyes away from Allen and focused them on the officer. He jumped forward to attack the officer, but his strike was deflected when the officer turned into a gnat.

Tomas stood there, confused. Then the officer turned back to his normal form and happily said, "I can turn into whatever I want just by imagining it. See?" The officer suddenly turned into Tomas, and he watched as Tomas stared. "Come on, you. I am one hundred percent you." The officer grinned.

"But let me make sure that you're not a fraud," Tomas said. "Stick out your hands. My hands are always cool, so if yours are cool, then you can kill me."

"Um, sure, yeah, sure," the officer stammered, obviously confused. He dropped his sword and held out both palms. Tomas reached his hands out as if to touch them, but instead he slashed the officer with his sword, cutting off his arms. The arms quickly started growing back in place, but Tomas pushed the officer over the railing and watched him go down, down, down into the lava.

Officer Hellmount looked back up with bold eyes and screamed from the fire, "I cannot die, Tomas Knight. I can see the past, future, and present, and you will regret going after anyone else. Bad things will happen everywhere you go. I will—" Before the officer could finish his sentence, he vanished.

Tomas took a deep breath and then turned to Allen. His face was now more pale than usual, and the strange black blobs were growing around his limbs and chest. Tomas had heard of what was happening to him. This was called the Darknelobe virus, and after a while it took over a person's body and killed him. Tomas knew that Allen had a day or so before it would happen, so he turned to the scene between General Ventex and Director Pierce.

Tomas saw that Director Pierce was hitting the general. He was about to step in and join the fight, when he saw a custos ball come rolling away from them. He picked it up and noticed that it was the general's custos ball from his golden sword.

Tomas looked over at the general and heard him whisper, "Smash it." Tomas did as he was told. He chucked the ball onto the walkway and then jumped back as the glass flew everywhere. The custos started growing rapidly.

Director Pierce turned around and gasped. The full-grown custos shrieked at him, causing him to fall back off the walkway. After shrieking, the custos slithered off the side of the walkway by accident. Tomas thought Director Pierce was gone, but he saw a pair of hands gripping the edge of the walkway.

Tomas walked over and helped the general up. After that, he went over to the dangling director and looked down at him. "I'm not burning alone," Director Pierce growled. Tomas stood there, frozen, but not knowing why.

Director Pierce held on to the edge of the floor with one hand and reached for Tomas's foot with the other. He was about to grab it and then let go of the ledge and fall into the fire with Tomas, but at the last second, Nathan put his foot in the way, causing Pierce grab him instead. Pierce fell backward, down into the fire, with Nathan's foot still in his hands.

"Nathan!" Tomas yelled. Tomas didn't take his eyes off of the two until there was nothing but lava left. Tomas looked over at his other companions about five feet away and saw that they all had blank faces. He heard the sound of soldiers coming down the stairs behind him, and then he heard the general say, "I'll hold them off. Now go. And Tomas, you are the one who was prophesied by Dondo. It is up to you to defeat a rising evil, and that evil is far worse than the Check army. It's a golem. Go!"

Tomas started running, and then he remembered Allen. He went back and picked Allen up and hoisted him over his shoulder. He ran back toward the gap, but he knew that with Allen's added weight, he wouldn't make it across. He pulled his grappling hook off his belt and fired it at a metal bar attached to the ceiling.

He made it back to the other side, but he noticed that Valery, Patrick, Teddy, and Freddy weren't there. Only Roger was there, and it seemed as if he wanted to see the general get killed. Instead he helped Tomas carry Allen.

By the time they got to the top of the stairway, parts of the building were starting to quickly fall apart. Tomas looked around for the others, but he didn't see them. They walked around, yelling their names, and were about to give up, when suddenly they heard the sound of yelling kids—not the yelling of fear but of freedom.

Tomas looked to his left and saw at least a thousand kids, all running. They ran right past Tomas and Roger, and when Tomas looked over to see where they were going, he saw only a docking bay—and *The Argovince* docked at the end of it.

Tomas watched with a grin as they all boarded it. He heard the engines start up again and watched it fly away, now taken over by children. Tomas walked off with Roger, and soon they saw the others emerge from the "5-20" room. They had broken all the locks and set the children free.

Patrick offered to carry Allen, which he did, because Roger was sore after carrying him up flights of stairs. They all ran over to the scoot and hopped onto it.

As they got back onto the platform, Tomas took a moment to reflect on what the officer had said before vanishing. What had he meant when he'd said that something bad would happen wherever Tomas went? He decided not to think about it.

He focused on the ground, which was now covered with crumbs of stone. After making it out of the final hall and into the courtyard, Tomas looked behind him into the hall and saw the columns collapsing on each other. They drove straight through the open doors and out of the hexagon.

Once they got to the ship, they gave their suits back to the soldiers who had been stuck in there for a couple of hours. They gave one of them a Nova Guard suit, because Pete had taken a Check uniform. After sending them off the ship and back to the scoot, the platform closed, and everything became silent. Roger and Patrick went to the bunkroom, and each hopped into a bunk. Valery went and started up the ship. Allen was placed onto the floor, and Freddy and Teddy started mending him. They seemed to know a lot about medicine.

Tomas went and sat down on a bench.

"So, Tomas, do you want to change the name of our ship?" Valery asked. "I mean, to me the current name is a bit girly."

Tomas thought about it for a while and then came up with a new name. "Let's call it *The Winter*," he said. "After all, Nathan's last name was Winter, and it would be a good memorial to him. It also sounds cool."

"Well," Valery said, "it looks like this is the start of *The Winter's* journey."

They painted "*The Winter*" on both sides of the ship and then painted a huge snowflake on the front of the ship.

Pete landed on Luminite only a day after he'd left the dying hexagon. He was there because he had finally gotten a blood sample of a night mare. He had gotten it when the children had gone off and left him, thinking he was dead.

Pete walked around the surface of Luminite for a while until he found what he was looking for. In front of him was a small wooden door built into the ground. He opened it, hopped in, and closed the door. "Finally, I have the last piece for my experiment to work. Soon it will all be worth it. It would have been a lot easier to do this if it hadn't been for Captain Freeman and his stupid heart attack. But hey, this is it."

Pete walked up to a desk that had been overtaken by cobwebs. He brushed them off the desk and opened it. Inside were nine golden custos balls. He grabbed them all, walked over to a control panel, slowly inserted all of them into the right places, and then carefully injected the blood sample into a tube. He was startled by the sound of the balls crushing, but he knew it was all part of the plan.

Above the control panel was a giant window, and Pete watched as the custoses fell out of their holders in the panel and into the room in front of him. He watched as they grew to their normal size. "Okay, now!" Pete said as he pressed a button.

The blood sample poured into the room with the custoses. It sprayed all over them. Pete waited for the moment when they would transform. And then they did start to transform—into exactly what Pete had expected. "This is it!" he said. Pete didn't know what he was getting himself into.

PART 2

For Peter Rack, life was going great. He had nine out of eleven custos balls and a night mare's blood sample. As he watched the custoses transform when the night mare's blood was poured on them, he was amazed. They were all binding together into one being, and from the looks of it, it would be dangerous and deadly—just how Pete wanted it.

As they finally finished binding together, Pete pressed a button that injected a sleeping gas into the room. The thing fell asleep, giving Pete a good chance to go and examine it. When he entered the room, he got to see the creature up close. It looked amazing. "The crystal golem," Pete said.

The beast was a tar-black creature with crystals sticking out of its spine. It looked like a bunch of rocks all stuck together. "With you, my friend, I can conquer the galaxy," Pete said. "I just need to keep playing it cool until those kids are *gone*."

Pete did like the kids, but he knew they might turn on him if they found out who he really had been before Fleet 404's crash. When the golem started shifting, Pete figured it would be best to leave the room. In fact, he decided to leave the bunker and sit down on Luminite's shiny white ground.

After a while, he started getting the feeling that he was being watched by someone or something in the distance, and he headed back into the bunker. After he closed the door above him, he turned around and almost screamed.

"Hello, Mr. Rack. I see you have created the golem."

Pete saw a scarred man with a peg leg. "What do you want, Officer?" he asked bitterly.

"I'm here for your creation. If I have it, I will be unstoppable,"

Pete looked down at his feet. "Well, I'm not going to give the golem to you without a fight," he said, pulling his sword out of his belt. He held it in front of him and ran toward the officer. At the last second, he jumped, thinking that he would hit the officer, but instead he fell straight on his back. He had gone right through the officer. "But … how did … no … it can't …" Pete stammered.

"As I told you, I am darkness, and darkness cannot be destroyed," the officer said.

"Well," Pete said proudly, "I'm willing to test that theory." He stood up, brushed himself off, and said, "I've survived one war. I'm not ready for another."

CHAPTER 6
The Spark of War

Tomas was starting to get bored after being on *The Winter* for numerous days. He tried to entertain himself by sorting things in the cargo hold, but that just made time go slower. He tried mending Allen a few times, but he always messed something up. He even tried suiting up and going out onto the roof a few times, but either he got blown off by solar winds and had to be rescued, or he got scared because of something moving in the shadows of space. One time he saw Patrick's custos, but he wasn't close enough to make out the details.

Patrick was having the same feelings Tomas was. He and Tomas usually talked to pass the hours, but Patrick soon had less and less to talk about. The only time he got really excited was when Valery painted his metal arm blue, but the paint started peeling off in the shower.

Allen was almost well. For the most part, he just slept. When he was awake, he only groaned and mumbled, as if he didn't know how to speak.

Valery was getting tired of driving the ship all day, and the only thing she'd enjoyed recently was painting Patrick's metal arm blue. No one knew where they were heading—not even Valery, who was usually in control of the ship.

Valery had made up her mind to go to Morinthia, a planet with no orbit and no solar system. It just floated in the gaps of space. She had done some research about the planet on a telaputer, which was pretty much the same as a computer but was more advanced. She found out that the planet was made of iron, nickel, copper, and steel. It was black-looking with some red and orange spots on it. She guessed that it had some inhabitants on it, and she was right.

Tomas woke up the next day feeling the same as he always did in the mornings on *The Winter*: drowsy. He asked Valery when they would be landing somewhere. She told him they were headed to Morinthia, because they sold fuel for a good price all over the planet, but first they were going to land on a barasteroid. Barasteroids were small towns built on the surface of asteroids. They usually had basic things for sale there, like food, beds, and maybe even ships or slaves. Tomas asked, "When are we going to be there exactly?"

"In about an hour," Valery said.

Tomas was thrilled that he would be able walk around somewhere and see other people and bargain a deal. He loved bargaining. Ever since he was little, he had always found it entertaining. He was also very good at it. For the next hour, Tomas couldn't stay still. He was like a little kid waiting for Christmas morning. He couldn't even speak right. He kept on stuttering whenever he talked because of the excitement.

Roger and Patrick seemed to be pretty happy too. They were not as hyped up as Tomas, but they were still excited. Freddy and Teddy seemed not to really care. They were still focused on mending Allen. Tomas knew that Allen would be all right, but he still worried about him sometimes. Allen had been his first friend back at the academy, and Tomas would hate to lose him.

"Okay, guys," Valery yelled from the cockpit. "We will be landing in about one minute. Suit up."

Tomas went to the closet in the bedroom and put on the black suit with the uncomfortable face mask that pressed up against his face. Roger, Teddy, and Patrick all did the same, but Freddy had to stay behind because of Allen. After the ship landed, Valery suited up, opened the platform at the end of the ship, and walked out with the others.

The platform closed behind them, and Tomas could see a town, but it was not what he'd expected. It was built out of old metal and rusted ships. Everyone there seemed to be miserable. They all wore gray suits that had a few holes in them, and when Tomas, Patrick, Teddy, Roger, and Valery passed them, the all held up cans. Tomas had seen this before: poor people begging and towns that seemed to have only outcasts as citizens. He hated the scene.

"Tomas and Roger, I want you to go back to the ship and get your swords," Valery whispered nervously.

Tomas didn't know what was going on. Why would they need swords in such a derelict town? Tomas looked around the town and suddenly saw what Valery was worried about. He saw two space pirates giving quick glances in their direction from about ten yards away. Tomas was afraid of space pirates, but after the incident in his dorm at the academy where the pirates had refused to attack, he felt a bit more confident. He and Roger did as they were told and ran back to the ship. The platform lowered and they walked inside, not bothering to close it behind them.

As they walked into the ship, they saw Freddy with vomit all over his shirt. Tomas soon realized that Allen had become sick. He went into the bunkroom, got his sword from his cot, and then headed back out to where the others were. They were still in the same place.

When Tomas and Roger caught up to them, Tomas saw that the pirates were only a few yards away, inching their way toward them. He and the others waited and stared until the pirates yanked out silver daggers and lunged toward them. Frozen with surprise, Tomas would have been hit by one of the daggers except that pirates fell to the ground at his feet. He looked down at them and saw that they had been shocked by something.

Tomas looked up to see what had happened, and he saw someone in a lightning-blue suit with a black face mask. The person was holding a small silver blaster and had multiple other blasters all over his suit.

Tomas and the others were speechless. The person put the blaster away, gave them a thumbs up, and ran away to a small Nova Guard craft—the same one that Pete had had on Frozer. The person jumped into the open cockpit and flew away into space toward Morinthia, which was now visible.

Tomas and Teddy went back to the ship, still in shock, while Valery and Roger went to buy food. When Tomas entered the ship, he told Freddy all about what had happened. Freddy had somehow burned his shirt with his sword and had gotten a new one from the cargo hold. Tomas got out of his suit and put it back in the closet. Soon after that, Roger and Valery came back.

Allen started becoming sick again, making the entire ship reek. Just to avoid the smell, Tomas suited up again and went up onto the roof with

Patrick. "So, Patrick, do you think my dad is looking for me right now?" Tomas asked as they sat on the roof.

"Maybe," Patrick said. "My folks gave me up for adoption when I was really little. I was adopted onto a family of soldiers on Luminite. While I grew up, my twelve brothers were all at war. It was the war that followed the Cosmic War thirty years ago. They weren't really my brothers, but I liked to think of them like that. They fought against the Check Army when it was just forming into something major. One day while they were fighting, though, something happened. They were fighting on Soleverya, a planet located between two stars, which makes its orbit a figure eight. Everything was going fine, and the Astro Army had the upper hand, when suddenly the cores of the stars collapsed at the same time, creating a hypernova. Only half of the Check Army was there, leaving the Astro Army with a disadvantage. Soleverya was right in the middle of the stars, which meant that every single atom was destroyed on that planet. After that, my parents wouldn't let me go to war, and they treated me like a baby until about a year ago. Then I went venturing off into the woods and found my former sword lying in the dirt. The reason I gave it up was because I have a metal arm now."

Tomas wasn't looking for a sad family story, just a one- or two-word answer, but he was okay with the story too. Suddenly he heard Valery's voice speaking in his face mask. "Tomas, you should probably come back down here right now. In about ten minutes we will be entering the atmosphere of Morinthia. Tomas looked up and gasped. In front of him was a planet at least two times the size of Earth.

"Wow," Tomas whispered to himself. After examining the vast planet, he headed back down into the ship. He decided to keep his face mask on because of the smell, but he put the rest of the suit away. Tomas ran up to the cockpit and sat down next to Valery to see the planet.

"Tomas, bring only your suit, not your face mask," Valery said. "The air here smells amazing. The academy took a trip here once when I was ten or something."

Tomas wondered if he would see here the person who had saved him back on the barasteroid. After he pondered this for a moment, he guessed that he wouldn't. But he was wrong. He discarded the thought when he saw an H-98 ship come toward them from Morinthia. This was the type of ship his father had.

"Maybe I should check in with that ship just to see if my father's on it," Tomas said jokingly to himself.

Edward Knight had been trying to find Tomas for almost a month now. He had put his son's picture on posters on the barasteroids, saying that there would be a great reward for whoever found him. He had canceled his archeology trips to look for Tomas. He had even contacted the Check Army's prisons to see if they had him, but he'd found nothing. Edward had felt completely responsible for Tomas's falling out of the ship. He had gone to many planets looking for him. He had even gone back to Frozer but had only found a Nova Guard bunker. He had just left Morinthia after finding nothing but a large Nova Guard ship passing him to go there. "Maybe I should check in with that ship just to see if Tomas is on it," Edward said jokingly to himself.

The Winter landed on small rocky hill. This time Teddy said that the Morinthian fresh air would be good for Allen, so they decided to bring him outside for a while.

When Tomas smelled the air, he coughed and gagged. The air smelled like fire and burned his lungs. "I … thought … you said … it smelled … good," Tomas said to Valery, still coughing."

"Yeah, yeah, at first it is kinda strange," she said, "but you get used to it after a few minutes."

Tomas held his breath and looked around at his surroundings. He then looked over toward Allen to see how he was doing. He heard Allen mumble, "I got to go."

"Oh, come on," everyone said simultaneously. Teddy walked Allen back inside and decided to just stay with him.

Everyone else started descending the small hill, following Valery, who seemed to know where they were. After walking for about half an hour, Tomas's lungs did get used to the air. They all walked in silence, until a small house came into view. As they got closer, they noticed a sign on the side of the house that said "Fuel. I+N"

Before Tomas could ask what "I+N" meant, Valery said, "Iron and nickel. Our ship's manual says it will only work with *Fe* and or *Ni* elements. Looks like we are in luck."

Tomas didn't know a lot about elements. He had always thought that the elements were earth, fire, water, and wind, but he was clearly wrong.

They entered the house but saw no one there. It was a plain wooden room that had lanterns lit on the walls. At the end of the room was a staircase spiraling downward. Above the staircase was a sign that said, "Fuel Mine." Tomas and the others knew that there were other words on the sign, but they didn't bother reading them. They headed down the staircase to see if anyone was down there to sell fuel to them. What they didn't read on the sign was, "Fuel Mine. Abandoned because of massive spiders."

They all grabbed lanterns, which were somehow still lit, and started walking single file down the spiraling stairs. After a minute or so, they came to a platform made of wood. The platform was about ten feet square and had small railings surrounding the sides.

Tomas looked around and decided to walk to the edge of the platform. He got to the railing and peered out. As he swung his lantern around, he noticed that the platform was above a large ravine. As he looked down into the blackness, he noticed more stairs going down and down. The platform was the only illuminated place in the entire ravine.

As they started heading down another set of spiraling stairs near the edge of the platform, Tomas heard a nonhuman screech from bellow. "Um, guys, what was that?" Tomas asked in a frightened tone.

"I dunno," Patrick said. "Could just be the echoes of a bat."

They kept heading down the stairs and reaching platforms for the next two hours. They stopped a couple of times to rest. The shrieks started becoming louder and louder. "I don't have a good feeling about this," Tomas said.

"Same here," Freddy said nervously. "Valery, I think we should turn back."

"We've come this far, so we may as well just go see what is at the bottom," she said.

"Valery, it's really obvious that no one is working down here," Tomas said in an agitated tone.

"But what about the weird screeching?" Patrick said.

"It's probably just some—" Valery was cut short by a soft humming sound deep below them. It was hard to hear, but they all stopped and listened. As they stood there, the humming got louder and louder. Then they saw it: in the far distance against the ravine wall was a small light, a lantern.

They all stood in silence until the humming stopped. The figure holding the lantern was most likely looking at them from the distance. They were about to start heading back up the stairs when the figure yelled, "Do not go any farther, for it is the Valley of Bones."

"What did it say?" Patrick said.

"Dunno," Tomas replied. They decided not to focus on the figure for a while, but then they heard the shriek again. They all frantically looked over at the lantern. They heard the figure yell and then fall silent. The lantern dropped from the figure and went tumbling down into the abyss.

As they kept walking down, they all started feeling cool. Tomas had experienced many different kinds of cold but never something like this. It felt good—cold but good. Tomas shone his lantern downward and saw a stone pathway. When they all got onto the pathway and off the stairs, they looked around. In front of them was a circular room with small openings in the sides. The openings were paths to somewhere. They stood in silence and then heard something from one of the corridors. Tomas shone his light into the corridor and screamed, which caused him to drop his lantern. In front of him was a spider the size of a good-sized room.

Tomas and the others stepped away from the creature, blasters and swords at the ready. The laser pins on the blasters helped Tomas aim where he wanted to shoot, but when he pulled the trigger, the laser bullet had no effect on the spider. It only pushed it back a little, giving Tomas and the others a chance to retreat back up the stairs.

The spider lunged at the stairs and went smashing through them, making Tomas and Patrick and Freddy to go flying off and onto the cold hard ground. Roger and Valery kept running up the stairs, but they decided to turn back for the others.

"Don't come back!" Tomas yelled to them. "Go!"

Valery gave him a worried look and then nodded, running back up the steps with Roger.

Tomas was now left in almost utter darkness, and he could see only a few feet in front of him. The spider lunged at them again, this time knocking Patrick back a few yards and sending Freddy running to the left to avoid the spider's attack. Tomas yelled to Patrick, who got up just in time to avoid being attacked by the spider again. Once they were all together again, they ran toward the closest corridor and down it. Tomas heard the spider shriek behind them and then start crawling after them.

But Tomas heard something else behind the beast. It sounded like rattling bones. A peacekeeper. No, many peacekeepers. An army of them. Tomas now heard shouting and footsteps emerging from every corridor. He didn't know that this was the beginning of something terrible.

They ran down the corridor for a couple of minutes, the sound of marching feet getting louder. Tomas didn't know why peacekeepers would be down here or why they had giant spiders. Freddy was afraid of the dark. Patrick was not so scared, because he had a metal arm, but he was not a big fan of spiders, especially ones that were larger than he was. They all kept running until they saw a dim light coming from around the bend. Then they heard humming, the same humming they had heard before. Tomas got his blaster ready, Freddy got his sword ready, and Patrick held up his metal arm on one side and a pistol in his other hand.

They slowly walked toward the sound, and then a figure turned the bend. They all pulled their triggers, and Freddy shot fire out of his sword. The figure seemed to be unaffected by the hits. It was transparent, a ghost that just floated there. It wore a scruffy beard, a miner's helmet, and overalls, but these too were not real.

"Who ... who are you?" Tomas asked, lowering his blaster.

"I am one of the many miners who perished down here," the ghost said. "This valley has a curse. When someone dies down here, his soul remains here until the end of time. We wander about, humming a certain song so we know where the others are. The screechers, those giant spiders, sometimes attack us. If we are attacked, we take their place as a spider, and the spider's soul is freed. Well, the spiders don't really have a soul. The peacekeepers somehow made them with dark magic, and they put our souls into them. It's pretty confusing, if you ask me. By the way, Azamore, the leader of the peacekeepers, is coming for you, so you'd better run. And remember, whenever you hear our hum, come and find us. We can always give help." Then the ghost vanished from sight.

Tomas was confused, but he kept on walking. As he walked, he heard a screech. Then he heard another, and another. Something was happening up ahead, and it didn't sound good. He slowed his run to a jog, just to be careful. He kept on tripping on bones on the floor, which really agitated him. The screeches kept getting louder, until he saw the source of the noise. At the end of the corridor was a giant room full of mine carts. In front of the carts was a track for them, which led down.

Tomas looked around and saw something huge—a screecher. This one was different, though. It had … a rider? In fact, the rider was a peacekeeper—with no hood. Tomas couldn't help but stare at the peacekeeper. He'd never seen what they looked like without their hoods on. This one had a skeleton's head. The peacekeepers were skeletons.

Tomas wished he could have studied it longer, but he couldn't because the spider lunged forward at him. He did not have time to move out of the way, but he was saved when Patrick leaped in front of him and knocked the spider hard with his metal arm. The peacekeeper went soaring off and shattered into pieces against the wall. The three companions hopped into the mine cart on the tracks and pushed off before the spider regained its wits. Tomas thought he was safe, but only for a moment.

Valery and Roger had made it about halfway up the spiraling stairs when they heard the sound of metal against flesh—not human flesh but spider flesh. They wondered what it was. Roger was tired of holding Patrick's lantern, which Patrick had given him before they separated. They both feared that Tomas and Freddy and Patrick were gone, but they still had a little bit of hope left.

They stopped at the nearest platform for a rest and sat for about five minutes, sweating because of the fast run up the stairs. They would have stayed longer, but then they heard a sound they had heard earlier that day: humming. It came from a figure that seemed to have been killed by one of the spiders. The humming was coming closer and above them. Someone was heading for them from above, maybe five stories up. But it wasn't a some*one*. It was more like a some*thing*.

Tomas, Freddy, and Patrick all headed lower into the darkness in the cart. Freddy had dropped his lantern when he'd hopped into the cart, and Patrick had given his to Roger. The only light they now had was the dimness of Freddy and Tomas's custoses because of the nearby peacekeepers, but that was very dim. The cavern seemed to be infested with peacekeepers. The glow of the custoses was not helpful enough to see where they were, but then Patrick told them, "You know that I have a built-in light in my metal arm?"

"You tell us this now?" Freddy yelled.

"Sorry. Geez, it's just a light," Patrick murmured.

Tomas looked over at Patrick's arm and saw that his metal palm was opening up to reveal a circle. The circle instantly lit up, illuminating about twenty feet all around them. Patrick could control the light with his mind. They noticed that there were wooden walls about ten feet to their left and a wall of glimmering crystals on their right.

"Quartz," Tomas said quietly to himself. He wanted so badly to hop out of the mine cart and collect some samples, but he decided that this would be a foolish move.

"Uh, guys? Where are we going?" Freddy asked.

Tomas realized that they did not know where they were going. "Well, all mine carts come to an end eventually, right?" he said.

"Guys!" Patrick yelled. Tomas and Freddy resumed looking forward and yelled too. There was a peacekeeper in the middle of the track up ahead—holding a blaster. Tomas heard the sound of it going off, closed his eyes, and then hitting something hard. And that was it.

Valery and Roger got their swords ready, and each held a small blaster as well. "Valery, try snapping," Roger whispered.

"Oh, yeah," Valery said stupidly. She put down her weapons and took off her gloves. She cracked her knuckles and then lifted one hand above her, where the whistling was coming from. She took a deep breath and pushed her figures together to make the snapping noise. She expected to hear the sound of someone falling down, which she did, but it wasn't the person coming toward them from above. It was Roger.

"Oh, come on!" Valery said, her face now a deep red. "How hard is it for things to go right for me for once?"

"Excuse me, but are you a mortal?" asked a gentle voice from behind her. "You don't sound like one of the peacekeepers."

Valery, her face now purple, spun around and fired a shot with her blaster.

"Do not be angry, child," the glowing figure said. "I sense that you have lost something and wish to find it—I mean *them*."

"How did you know?" Valery asked, her face turning its normal pale color again.

"I see many things, child," the ghost said. "I am not living; I am simply dead. Well, my body is. My soul must remain here till the end of time, for this valley is cursed. If you die, then your soul may not move on to the heavens. We cannot leave."

"Why ... why did you become a ghost?" Valery asked, cocking her head slightly.

"Well, child, sit, and I will tell you of the tale."

Valery, who always loved a good action-packed tale, sat on her knees.

"It all began many years ago right here," said the ghost. "I and many other men worked down here, mining for iron and nickel. One day, ships started using solar power. They had done so before, but they'd always needed a bit of fuel in case was no sun where they were. Once people figured out how to harness solar power throughout the cosmos, we had no purpose. We were all packing up and getting ready to leave, when the Cosmic War started. This was when the Check Army had just been formed and the ancient peacekeepers had been found again. They were first sent here to kill the population so the Check Army would have complete control over the planet. They wanted it for its natural resources, and it just so happened that when those skeleton soldiers—peacekeepers—came here to invade, the mine was their first stop.

"When they came down here, we fought to the end. All of us died except for one lucky soul: William Pierce. He was just a boy. Don't know why he was down here; he just was. He escaped and stole one of the massive warships brought by the peacekeepers, all by himself. Must have been about your age: fifteen. We never heard from him again, but I learned that he converted the warship into an academy. Anyway, the leader of the peacekeepers, Azamore, made this their dwelling. They somehow made giant spiders that only worked if they had a human soul in them. If you see any big spiders, it is one of us, but we cannot control ourselves once in their bodies. So I urge you to get out of here and never come back."

Valery looked down into the ravine and then at the ghost. "Looks like I have no choice."

Tomas woke up in a room lit with dim candles. He tried to walk, or even move, but he soon realized that he was tied to a wall with chains. Patrick and Freddy were tied up next to him, looking around. "What happened?" Tomas said.

"A peacekeeper shot our cart," Freddy answered in a bored tone. "We went flying out. You hit a wall. I hit the peacekeeper. Patrick lost his arm."

"Wait, what?" Tomas said, trying to look over at Patrick's arm.

Patrick just held out a stump that protruded from his shoulder. The metal arm was gone. Tomas got a good look at Patrick. His suit was all torn up from hitting something, which had clearly taken his arm clean off.

"Yup, and now I'm mad," Patrick said. They stood there in silence for a moment. Then they heard footsteps coming from the dark hall in front of them. Tomas had not yet gathered all of his wits back after the mine cart incident, but he had enough sense to know whom those footsteps belonged to. They were the light but kind of crunchy, the footsteps of a peacekeeper, and from the sound of it, there were most likely many of them.

As the first one came into view, Tomas noticed that it was not wearing the traditional black garb of the peacekeepers but instead was wearing a long golden cloak that dragged along the floor behind it. Under the cloak, which was open in the middle, was a breastplate that gleamed silver. It had most likely been created by the peacekeepers, because it had no details on the front. It was just a plain silver plate that covered its chest. Tomas recognized the metal. It was palladium, a very strong metal. Behind the peacekeeper with the golden cloak was an entire posse of normal peacekeepers, all looking like they were hoping to shed the blood of their captives.

"Greetings, mortals," said the leader of the peacekeepers. "I am Azamore of Borax."

"What's Borax?" Freddy asked.

"Borax is my kingdom—*was* my kingdom," Azamore said. "We peacekeepers have names and titles." Azamore held up a sword. "But after I was rid of my life by this very sword, I became a god. I have an army of soldiers now, and we are preparing to break away from Check control and start our own empire."

Tomas had decided to keep quiet—until Azamore drew his golden sword. "What are you going to do with us?" Tomas asked quietly.

"Well ... my spiders need to be fed too."

Valery had a tough time carrying Roger up the stairs. She had made it up to the next platform in an hour, which was slower than normal. The ghost had kept her company, but Valery was starting to get tired of listening to him talk about different kinds of rocks. "Excuse me, Mr. Ghost, no hard feelings, but you're kinda starting to get on my nerves," she said with the slightest bit of exasperation in her voice.

"Oh, of course, Ms. Valery," the ghost said, sounding almost happy. He vanished, leaving only an empty lantern behind.

Valery looked up and saw the dim light of the shack above. She kept on climbing until she heard voices up ahead—in the shack. It couldn't be a ghost, and as far as Valery knew, peacekeepers couldn't talk without vocal cords. So, who else could it be? The voices sounded human, and she couldn't help listening.

"We should go now, ma'am," said a voice above Valery. "We have picked up signals of life down there."

"No," a woman's voice replied. "Azamore and his armies are down there, and you know what he is waiting for."

"I do not, ma'am," the first person said.

"He is waiting for us to come down so he can kill us and use our weapons. The Nebula Corps depends on us exterminating the peacekeepers before they go to Luminite to join Officer Hellmount and start an empire—one that cannot be destroyed."

Valery would have stayed on the steps and listened longer, but she felt someone's hand touch her shoulder. She spun around, expecting Roger, but instead it was a person dressed in a lightning-blue suit with blasters all over his body.

"Come on," said the stranger. "It is not safe down here."

Valery stood up and walked up the few remaining steps into the shack. The person who had touched her shoulder carried Roger. Valery froze when she saw the people in front of her, all giving her strange looks.

"Um … hi," Valery said, not knowing what else to say.

"Hello, child," said a tall woman. "Please do not be afraid. I am Madam Pofer, and I am the leader of the Nebula Corps, not the Nova Guard. We are going through quite a poser right now, so if you would, just follow Sergeant Wilson back to our ship, and then … Oh, man, I didn't think this part through. Okay, how about you just stay with us in this shack and just don't talk, all right?"

Valery wanted to know more about these people, but she decided to be quiet, as requested. Still, she had too many questions boiling up inside her. "My friends are down there!" she screamed suddenly. "You need to go down right now! And why are you called the Nebula Corps? You should be fined with that law—you know what I'm talking about! You are a rip-off of the Nova Guard."

"The Nova Guard finds swords," Madam Pofer said bitterly. "We are a well-organized army. Okay, sergeant, take the brat back to the ship. And give her some food. She must be very hungry." Valery was led out of the shack by a tall, bald, dark-skinned man. When she got outside, she expected to see a small ship that was falling apart, but she saw a whole lot more. There were massive gray ships, the smallest being the size of a football field. Nebula Corps soldiers were running about with crates, hovering tanks, giant drills with wheels, and even smaller Nova Guard crafts. Valery could have stared at the scene for hours, but she was pushed forward by the sergeant.

"Say hello to your new home," he said with a smile. "You will like it."

Only seconds after Valery left, Madam Pofer sent thousands of soldiers down into the ravine. She kept Roger in the room for no reason. She herself, suited up in a lightning-blue suit, went down into the ravine. She had already thought through the part about getting down there using rocket boots. As all the Nebula Corps soldiers went down into the ravine, they kept on hearing screeches.

"Custoses," Amber said to Madam Pofer. Amber was only fifteen but was qualified for her job.

"Yes, most likely," Madam Pofer said. They all kept going down for about ten minutes until they reached the ground. Soldiers looked at their human-tracker devices and saw three signals coming from one of the corridors near them. They all walked in single file down the corridor until they got to a place where mine carts were lined up, all facing a black tunnel—a mine shaft. They all walked down it, thousands of soldiers.

Azamore and some other peacekeepers had taken Tomas's and Freddy's swords and blasters. Patrick did not have anything to take, so they just pushed him aside. After that, the three boys were led down countless stairs and into a small room where they were given small bronze daggers. Tomas heard the roar of a crowd just outside the room, and he now knew what was to happen to them. Azamore and the other peacekeepers left the boys there with only the roar of the crowd.

"What now?" Tomas asked. The wall in front of him then opened, answering his question. Once the wall was fully open, Tomas saw a thin layer of sand covering the surface beyond the wall. They slowly stepped out into a torch-lit arena and looked up at a roaring crowd of cloakless peacekeepers. Once they were out of the room, the wall closed behind them.

Tomas looked around. He was in a massive, circular arena. At the opposite side of the arena was another wall, which was now opening. Tomas, Patrick, and Freddy stepped back. They could make out the shape emerging from the wall opening. It was a screecher—a big one. It started coming toward them slowly, then picked up speed, and finally came toward them at a run. The screecher had a rider.

"What now, Tomas?" Patrick asked.

"We prove ourselves." Tomas broke into a sprint, leaving the others behind. The screecher screeched and approached to within fifteen feet of Tomas. At the last moment, Tomas jumped up, his dagger ready in his hand. When he landed on the spider's head, he gripped his knife in both hands, pointed it at the spider's massive head. Then he plunged his dagger straight into the spider's head, causing black blood to go oozing everywhere. The screecher's violently shaking body whipped the rider off and into the stone wall, leaving him motionless.

Patrick and Freddy, who had also leaped onto the beast and started violently slashing it, soon met up with Tomas. The spider screamed in pain, and Tomas yelled with joy. The spider was being stabbed to death by three boys with small bronze daggers, but clearly the spider was not just going to let them win. It jumped up and did a barrel roll, and when it landed, it nearly crushed Tomas. Patrick and Freddy fell off onto the sandy ground.

Patrick got up and ran back to the spider, and sliced one of its legs, but Freddy had twisted his ankle and had trouble getting up. Tomas noticed Freddy's difficulty and was about to get off the spider and help him—but the spider was quicker.

Sergeant Wilson led Valery onto one of the larger ships and into a cafeteria that was about the size of the one back on the academy. "You may get anything you wish, Ms. Valery," he said proudly.

"What?" Valery asked, confused.

"Watch," the sergeant said. He walked over to a table holding plates and cups. "Orange juice," he said.

To Valery's delight, one of cups filled up with orange juice.

"Now, Ms. Valery, you cannot wish for anything extreme, like purple milk. You can wish for the basics, like soda, juice, water, and normal milk. It works the same way for the food. You stay here and wish up some food, and I will be right back." The sergeant scurried out of the room, leaving Valery alone.

She walked up to the cups and said, "Purple milk." Nothing. "Red milk." Nothing, "Come on. Can I at least have green milk?" Still nothing. "*Milk!*" Valery shouted. "How hard is it just to brew up some colorful milk?" The cup filled up with normal cold milk, which Valery drank.

Then she went over to the plates. "Ice cream. Chocolate ice cream." To her surprise, chocolate ice cream appeared on the plate. "Uh, purple milk," Valery said, hoping it would work. Nothing. "How about some caramel apples and a hot dog?" The plate now had a caramel apple, a hot dog, and chocolate ice cream. She went and sat down at one of the tables and happily wolfed down her food. After she was full, she brought her plate over to the place where she'd found it, and one last time she asked for purple milk … and it worked.

"My God," Valery said with a smile. She chugged down the purple milk and then burped loudly.

"Everything okay?" said a voice behind her.

Valery recognized the voice. "Sorry, Sergeant Wilson," she said.

"It's okay," he said. "Come now, you have visitors."

Valery didn't have a clue as to who it could be, but she was about to find out. She followed the sergeant down a hall until they got to a door. The door opened, and Valery stepped into the room. Someone was standing about twenty feet from her, facing away from her.

"Hello, Valery," the person said. "Do you remember me? Don't scream. If you do, I will kill you."

"Wait, who are you?" the sergeant yelled. "Valery, get behind me. Guards!" The sergeant pulled out a pistol and aimed it at the figure. "Show yourself!"

"That will be unnecessary, sir," the person said.

Valery watched in fright as the person turned around. She saw a pure black sword in the person's hands. Other Nebula Corps guards came into the room with weapons. The person took off his cloak and tossed it aside. It was Mr. Gaffen. He had survived the hexagon. He stared at everyone and then stabbed his sword into the ground, causing the ground to shake. Then, along with the shaking, metal from the floor came up perfectly, killing dozens of soldiers.

"Go, Valery. Run," the sergeant whispered. Valery ran, giving one glance back at him and the remaining soldiers. Mr. Gaffen was laughing now because of the misfortune of the soldiers. Their bullets and lasers seemed to be ineffective against his sword, which he used to block them.

Valery sprinted down the hall, not knowing what was going on. How had Mr. Gaffen lived? Only she and her six companions—and the other kids from the academy—had lived when the hexagon was destroyed. What did he want? Valery turned every corner she could find, and she soon came to an opening to the outside. She ran and screamed. Once she was a safe distance away from the ship, she looked back, fearing the worst for everyone inside. She watched as many soldiers ran into the ship with many weapons.

She ran back to *The Winter*, which was nearby. She opened the door and found Teddy and Allen playing cards.

"What happened out there, Valery?" Teddy asked.

"The spark of war," Valery said.

Tomas and Patrick stared at the spider and what it had just done. "It killed Freddy," Patrick whispered. "It actually killed him."

"Patrick, give me your dagger," Tomas said crossly.

Patrick handed it over to Tomas. "Give that beast what it deserves," he said.

Tomas nodded and ran up to the beast. He jumped up onto its back, put his and Patrick's daggers together, and cut. He was cutting a straight line in the spider's back and was yelling as he did it. He looked up at the place in the stands were Azamore was seated, and he could tell he was angry. Tomas wanted to somehow tease him, but he was soon flung off of the spider's back by something hitting him in the spine.

Tomas lay on the ground and looked up. He saw some rocks fall off of the spiders back. The crowd had been throwing rocks at him because they wanted him to die. The spider now turned to Tomas, being done with its last victim and still hungry. It slowly crept up to him, its massive black-and-yellow body towering over him, creating a dark shadow.

Tomas reached for the daggers, but he couldn't find them anywhere. They were still in the spider's back. Tomas wanted to scurry away from the screecher, but he couldn't.

The spider now leaned over him and brought one of its strange, knifelike legs up into the air right over Tomas. He screamed, knowing it was the end of the line for him, but to his surprise, the spider just fell to the ground, motionless.

Tomas looked around, trying to find out what had happened, and when he looked back at the wall they had come through, he saw people in lightning-blue suits running into the arena and firing into the crowd. The spider had been shot by one of the soldiers.

Tomas thought the crowd would flee, but instead they all grabbed their swords and ran down into the arena. The peacekeepers charged and collided with the lightning-blue soldiers. Tomas and Patrick ran back to the wall where they had entered. They were almost there when someone suddenly stopped them.

"Stop, children," the person said. "I am Madam Pofer. You are not safe in here. You shall be escorted back to the surface by this fine young lady." She pointed to a girl close to her.

Tomas smiled, and he headed out of the arena with the girl and Patrick.

Once they were safely out and heading back along the rail tracks again, the girl said, "Let's share some small talk. I'm Amber. I'm fifteen. I grew up on Earth." Amber had flaming red hair and pale skin with freckles.

"Uh, hi. I'm Tomas," he said awkwardly. "I'm also fifteen. I grew up on Hera."

"And how about you, armless boy?" Amber said to Patrick.

"I'm Patrick," he said. "I'm fifteen. I grew up on Luminite."

Tomas looked back at the glimmering walls full of quartz. He was about to go and cut some off with his sword when he remembered … he didn't have it. "Amber, Patrick, wait right here," he said. "I'll be back in a flash. I've lost one sword, and I'm not losing another."

He started running back down the mine shaft, when he heard Amber say, "Tomas, you might want this." She tossed him a small blaster, and Tomas nodded. He turned around to start running and then heard her again.

"And Tomas, don't get yourself into any trouble. Madam Pofer would be a bit frustrated."

Tomas nodded again and darted off.

"Sir, who is he?" Bobby Tyler asked the sergeant as they were shooting at Mr. Gaffen.

"I don't know, but he is too strong for us," Sergeant Wilson said. "He even stopped a shot from a rocket launcher with his sword. We cannot beat him."

"What are you suggesting, sir?" Bobby said.

"We only have one choice, Bobby. We must retreat." He held up one hand and screamed, "Retreat!" Everyone ran out of the room except Wilson and Bobby.

"Who are you, and what do you want?" Wilson said with an angry tone.

"I am just a man named Luke Gaffen," Mr. Gaffen said.

"What do you want?" the sergeant asked.

"That is simple," Gaffen said. "I have come here to start a war that needs to be fought."

"No war needs to be fought," Bobby said.

"This one does," Mr. Gaffen said. He held his sword out toward Bobby and added, "But how will you be able to fight it from beyond the grave?"

"Bobby, look out!" Wilson said.

Mr. Gaffen had fired a beam of light from his sword, and if Bobby hadn't jumped out of the way, the beam surely would have hit him. "Go, Bobby! Run!" Wilson shouted.

"Sir, I'm not leaving you here," Bobby said. He pulled another blaster from his belt and fired it at Mr. Gaffen. Once again, Gaffen blocked it and said loudly, "It's not the size of the dog in the fight; it's the size of the fight in the dog." He fired another beam of light from his blaster.

This time, Gaffen's aim was true. It hit Bobby right in the chest, knocking him back. Sergeant Wilson ran over to him and noticed that Bobby was starting to fade because the beam had hit him.

"Bobby, don't you die," the sergeant said.

"Sorry, sir," Bobby said, "but this is what was supposed to happen. It's for the best. Now go. You don't stand a chance. He's too strong. Please, sir, go." By the time he had finished speaking, he had fully faded, leaving nothing but metal floor where he had been.

"You took my friend," Wilson said to Mr. Gaffen. "Bobby was like a brother to me, and you took him. You will pay, but not now." He turned around and ran back down the hall. He picked up his telamonotor and said loudly, "Everyone evacuate ship number 651. I repeat, evacuate ship

651." He glanced back at Mr. Gaffen and saw him staring at him happily, as if he knew something that Sergeant Wilson didn't. Then he turned back around and kept running.

Mr. Gaffen wore a black-and-gray leather jumpsuit with shoulder pads strapped around his arms. The pads were triangles with bent points, making sharp vertexes that stuck out. Black kneepads were built in, and he had been holding a mask in his free hand the entire time. He put it on. The section in front of his eyes was red, which caused him see a red tint to everything, and the rest was black. He put his black sword back onto his belt and walked out of the room littered with badly wounded or dead soldiers. He laughed at the sight and kept walking.

"Just an evening stroll," he told himself, still chuckling. Mr. Gaffen then took something off his belt and tossed it to the ground. Once on the ground, it shot out a beam of light that Mr. Gaffen walked into. He was teleported by the light onto a Check warship over Luminite. He wanted to see if his old friend would want to pay him a visit.

Tomas ran down the shaft for a few minutes, and then he saw it: a small opening built into the wall. This was where he had come through with Amber and Patrick. He jogged down the hall until he heard the roar of battle not far away. He eventually came to the place where he had been chained up only about an hour ago. He walked farther that way until he came to a door that led to the arena's seating. He ran through that and into the stands. He looked down at the battle, and his smile turned into a frown. His heart sank. The peacekeepers had the upper hand. There were more of them, and they just kept on coming.

"Good job, boy. Even I was impressed," someone said from behind Tomas. Tomas knew the voice.

"Give me back my sword, Azamore," Tomas said, turning around. Azamore had enjoyed watching the Nebula Corps being killed.

"Why do you deserve it?" Azamore asked.

"Why do you need it?" Tomas said.

"Don't you think that we peacekeepers sometimes lose our swords too?" Azamore said. "I will give it back if you do me a favor. It is very simple. Someone down there is named Madam Pofer. I despise her. If you cut her life short, then I will give you your sword back."

"How will I do it?" Tomas asked.

"With this." Azamore held up a double-bladed ax with a diamond edge. Tomas looked around.

"Consider it done." He grabbed the ax and headed down to the battle in the arena.

Once Tomas was out of Azamore's way and in the arena, Azamore was greeted by a peacekeeper.

"Sir, what if he does it?" a peacekeeper asked.

"He's not getting his sword back," Azamore said. "It's already been destroyed and melted into crystal goo. I'll just have to kill him. He is of no use alive. And if he does not succeed, then he will die anyway when Hellmount returns with our secret weapon: the crystal golem."

CHAPTER 7
How the Fleet Crashed

Pete sat on the cold floor of the bunker for hours, not completely sure of what had just happened. "How did he get the golem?" Pete said quietly to himself. Pete had put up a real fight, but he was no match for Officer Hellmount. "Well," he said, "someone else needs me right now. With Gaffen alive, I may as well go to Morinthia."

Pete waited a few weeks before leaving, but once he was ready, he headed outside to where his Nova Guard craft was. He opened the cockpit and jumped in. "Azamore cannot get his hands on that golem," he said. He flew away from Luminite, having no reason to be there now.

As he was leaving the atmospheres, he saw a shadow behind one of the clouds. Then he saw it again. He decided to speed up his craft, not wanting to get in the way of whatever it was. He had almost made it out of the atmosphere, when the thing came flying at his craft. Pete yelled and turned around. He now saw that it was a night mare. "Those aren't in these parts!" he yelled. Someone had put it here purposely.

Then from above him, a Queen-4430 darted toward him, firing wildly. Pete had a hard time dodging the shots and was eventually hit. His craft went spiraling toward the ground. Sparks flew everywhere in back of him, and Pete knew there was only one solution: to jump. The crash would surely kill him, but jumping in a suit with a parachute might give him a chance.

Pete opened the cockpit, unbuckled, and jumped. He went soaring down, until he pulled his parachute. He landed on the ground safely, but only moments later, the night mare snatched him by the arms and carried him up. Pete had been going up for at least ten minutes when he then saw it—a Check warship. Pete was now a captive of the Check Army.

Tomas hopped into the arena with the double-bladed ax and headed toward the fight. He wasn't actually going to kill Madam Pofer, but he wanted Azamore to believe that he was. The ax was very light and quick-moving, and at its tip was a small metal spike. Tomas headed toward the peacekeepers but was interrupted by a familiar screech.

"Everyone get back!" someone yelled. Tomas was almost trampled by the retreating soldiers and was soon left in the dust with the Nebula Corps behind him. In front of him were three screechers—with wings. These massive spiders could up fly.

Tomas was between the two battling armies. He was just about to run back to the soldiers when the spiders leaped up into the musty air. As they were about to land on Tomas, he felt himself being pulled back by his arms. He looked back to see who it was, and he saw two Nebula Corps troopers pulling him back into the crowd of soldiers. The spiders landed where Tomas had been only moments before.

"Move out!" Tomas heard a woman say. All the soldiers started running back through the wall opening and back up the stairs. The peacekeepers didn't seem to care that their enemies were escaping.

Once everyone was out of the arena, Tomas had an idea that did not involve getting his sword back. A Nebula Corps trooper flew Tomas to the surface where he found Roger, who was sleeping for some reason. Then he saw Patrick and Amber. He met up with them and asked Amber a very serious question.

"Hey, Amber, you don't happen to have any custoses that are in their glass balls on your ships, do you?" Tomas asked. He was very impressed by the grand display of ships located near the false fuel shack, and he couldn't help asking.

"We do, yes," Amber said with a smile. "But they are hidden away very well in our cargo ship. I would never be able to get you one. But there is someone else who might. His name is Sergeant Wilson, and he is second in command in our unit. First is Madam Pofer. I'll see if he can get you one."

"Tomas, what do you want with a custos ball?" Patrick asked suspiciously.

"I'm going to try something never tried before," Tomas said, walking back toward *The Winter*.

The night mare dropped Pete onto a platform the size of a football stadium. The platform stuck out from the ship, and Pete could tell that it was a docking station. There were Queen-4430s all around him. Pete was about to steal one, when suddenly he heard someone yell, "Freeze! Put your hands up!" Pete put his hands up.

"Hello, Peter Rack. Do you remember me?" Pete turned around and saw someone he'd never thought he would see again. He had fought alongside Pete in the Cosmic War, but one day he'd decided to join the Check Army as a solar lord. They had been the best of the best with their swords, and they could almost never be defeated.

"Lukas Gaffen," Pete said. "I never thought I would see you again."

"Hellmount has the golem, I have you as a captive, and my men are going to be landing on Morinthia any minute to finish what I have started," Mr. Gaffen said. "And don't think your little friends will come for you, because they won't. You will soon be on Morinthia too."

The entire ship turned clear red, and suddenly Pete was on a ship over Morinthia. The Queen-4430s were getting ready to leave the landing platform for the ground.

Tomas headed back to the ship with Patrick, while Amber went to find Sergeant Wilson. She had trouble finding him in all the ruckus, and she decided to give up once she found out that a solar lord had almost killed him. She figured that he would not be in the mood to help her, so she just headed in the direction that Tomas and Patrick had headed.

While she was walking to *The Winter,* Amber felt something in her suit pocket. She opened it, having forgotten what it was, but when she saw it, she gasped. She had picked it up during the fight when one of the peacekeepers had fallen. It was a custos ball.

She ran to *The Winter* with a heavy heart, but when she got to it, she was amazed. The ship was nothing like she'd expected it to be. It was a black-and-red cube with two huge machine guns and some small blasters attached to the sides. Amber knocked on the side of the ship to see if anyone was there, and soon she heard the sound of metal touching the ground from the other side of the ship. She figured that this was the opening, and she walked into the ship. There her eyes met a strange sight. Nearest to her was a girl hugging Tomas, and in back of Tomas and the girl was a kid playing cards with Patrick. Amber heard sobbing to her far left, but she decided not to investigate. Only moments later, another person walked into the ship.

"Roger, you woke up," the girl said. "And Tomas, who's this other girl?"

"Oh," said Tomas. "Valery, that's Amber. Amber, this is Valery. Those two playing cards over there are Patrick—well, you know him—and Allen. The guy who just woke up is Roger. The person in there crying is Teddy. He just lost his brother. Don't bring it up."

There was an awkward moment of silence, but then Amber remembered why she was there, and she pulled the custos ball out of her pocket.

Tomas took it from her and examined it. "Wait one moment," he said, and he scurried off to the cargo hold. When he came back only a few minutes later, the custos ball had been successfully attached to the butt of his ax. Tomas could hardly believe his luck. It had worked. He could have stared at it all day, but he was interrupted by the smell of smoke not far off. He walked outside and saw where the smoke had come from. The entire fleet of Nebula Corps ships was engulfed in fire.

Tomas looked around with an open mouth to see what was happening, and then he saw it. At least two thousand Queen-4430s were flying over the fleet, all seeming to have a particular target: the cargo ship.

"They're here for the custoses," Amber said.

"Well, if they are, then let's go make sure that doesn't happen," Tomas said. They all headed back down the hill, except for Teddy and Allen, who was still not feeling well.

When Tomas got to the base of the hill, he heard a roar from above him. He looked up and frowned. It was a Check warship. He didn't know what to do. He surely could not defeat this mass of Check ships alone, and the weakened Nebula Corps would not help him do it. He had only one idea. "Guys, I need you all to stay behind and hide somewhere safe," Tomas said.

The others didn't know what he was talking about, but they ran back up the hill where the ship was and hid behind some boulders.

Tomas, on the other hand, ran toward one of the small shuttles only about a hundred feet away from him. He opened the cockpit and started it up. His plan was to go up to the Check warship and … well, he didn't know why, but he had a feeling that something up on the warship was important. As Tomas lifted off, he saw all of his friends hidden behind the boulders.

As Tomas got closer to the warship, he realized that all of the Queen-4430s weren't coming for him. He smiled and kept flying upward, not knowing the danger that lay ahead.

Tomas found an empty landing platform sticking out of the side of the warship. Only two figures were walking around the platform, and they were looking at each other. Tomas focused his vision on one of them and gasped. It was Pete.

Tomas flew forward and landed on the platform. He opened the cockpit and jumped out. He walked toward Pete and the other person, thinking that the other person was on Pete's side.

"Hello," Tomas yelled. Pete and the other person both quickly turned around, surprised that he was there. "Tomas!" Pete yelled from about fifty feet away. "Tomas, you have to go right now!"

"Quiet!" barked the person facing Pete.

"Pete, who is that?" Tomas called, still walking forward.

"I am Luke Gaffen, but I like to be referred to as a solar lord," the other man said.

"Pete, what's going on?" Tomas said, now only about twenty feet away from the two.

"It's a long story, Tomas," Pete said. "Now go back. It's not safe for you here."

"Oh, he won't have to leave just yet," the solar lord said. He pulled out a black sword and aimed it at Tomas, and suddenly a beam of light fired at him. He dodged it by a mere inch and decided that Pete needed his help.

Tomas drew his ax from his belt, pointed it at Mr. Gaffen, and charged him. Tomas was surprised when a green ball went whizzing from the front of his ax and headed straight toward Mr. Gaffen. Pete dove out of the way just in time for the green ball to hit Mr. Gaffen. When it hit him, the ball expanded around his body, making a massive green dome around him. Tomas walked over to Pete and stared at the dome with Mr. Gaffen trapped inside.

"Let me out this instant," Mr. Gaffen demanded from inside the green dome. Tomas had trouble hearing him because his voice was muffled by the green barrier surrounding him.

"Tomas," Pete said, "how did you do that? Only swords have that power."

"Well, some guy named Azamore kinda took my sword," Tomas said, "and if I wanted to get it back, I would have had to kill some lady I didn't know. He gave me this ax to do the job, but instead some girl named Amber gave me a custos ball, and I just attached it to the ax. So, yeah."

"And you were able to create an atom breaker?" Pete said.

"What?" Tomas asked.

"An atom breaker is what you shot out of your ax at Luke Gaffen," Pete explained. "After it hits someone or something, it creates a large, green dome around it. After about five minutes, it expands and then forces itself inward to make it smaller—until the thing inside is crushed. In the end, the atom breaker is about the size of one atom. That's how it got its name. But Tomas, it is almost impossible to create one of those with the custos's power. I had nine swords—all with extreme power—that couldn't do that. I decided to get rid of the swords, but I kept the custoses for experimental reasons."

"So, what are you suggesting?" Tomas asked.

"Tomas, that ax has more than two powers; it has *millions*. Your ax has the power of a golden sword."

Tomas did not want to see what was going to happen to Mr. Gaffen, so he and Pete ran over to a small door at the end of the landing dock that led to the engine room—at least that was what the writing on the door said. When they opened the door, they saw no one, which was good for the occasion.

"Pete, I have a question," Tomas said as they entered the engine room.

"What is it?" Pete said, looking around.

"Why did you leave us back at the hexagon?"

"I had some important business," Pete said.

"What was it?" Tomas asked.

"I knew this day would come," Pete replied. "Tomas, remember how I said I had nine swords with extreme power? Well, those were golden swords. Only eleven have ever been forged. My ancestors tracked the nine down throughout time. We did this because of Dondo's prophecy: "When a boy is lost but then found, he will never forget the sound of roaring motors and blasting guns. He will find one but will lose that too. The second will come, but will be burned into crystal goo. When the last one arrives, this boy will strive to keep his team alive. In the end, he, plus three, will defeat someone even more powerful than me. When *The Winter*'s crew rolls away, this boy will go back home for the rest of his days." Then Pete added darkly, "Tomas, I have finally created a crystal golem."

Tomas didn't know what this was, but judging from the prophecy, he guessed that it was not something to be happy about. He now got to take a good look at the engine room. It was about the size of six football fields. It had a massive generator in the middle, with fumes and steam pumping out of the bulky machine. There were stairways leading in all directions all over the place. Tomas liked the sight of it all, but then he saw something he didn't like. In fact, he despised it. "I thought I killed you," he said to the thing about a hundred yards away.

"Didn't I tell you that I cannot die?" the thing said. "And did you really think I would fall for that trick about your having cool hands? How were you supposed to feel the temperature of my hands with gloves on?" The thing continued. "And Mr. Rack, don't think I have forgiven you for crashing Fleet 404."

"I didn't crash it," Pete said angrily. "Captain Freeman ordered everyone out of the room so he could concentrate, and when I went to check on him when we started to enter the exosphere of Frozer, he had somehow had a heart attack. It was too late to change directions, and the parachutes wouldn't stop us. We would have hit the ground anyway. I knew that at least one sword had to be saved, so I ran to the cargo hold and jumped."

"Well, I do not think that's true," said Officer Hellmount, "so I am going to have to punish you with your own experiment." A massive golem with crystals all over it came out from behind the generator and made a very loud roar at the two. "Get ready to pay the price, Peter."

Amber, Valery, and Roger were the only ones still hiding behind boulders. Patrick had decided to go back to the ship because his arm was hurting, and he figured that he would be of no use to them without his sword or his metal arm.

As the three crouched there and watched the terrible scene, Amber proposed an idea. "How about we fly your ship up to the warship where Tomas is and try to destroy the main power source?" she asked.

Valery replied, "I've studied that kind of ship before. They are Narmarian warships. They have a massive generator near one of the landing platforms—docking bays, if you will. If we can fly *The Winter* up there and blast open the hull of the ship, then we will have a clear shot at the generator to destroy the warship. But the peacekeepers will be coming up soon. I can tell that they've been waiting for this for a while."

They all ran back to *The Winter* and started it up. Patrick had duct-taped a piece of wood with a fork at the end to the place where his metal arm should have been. Allen seemed back to normal and was now drinking a glass of milk. Teddy had become furious with the peacekeepers and was gathering all the weapons he could find to make some type of bomb. The ship started up without a problem, and within a minute it was near the warship.

"Tomas, you need to get out of here now!" Pete yelled to Tomas, even though he was only a foot away.

"I'm not leaving without you," Tomas said.

"So be it," Pete whispered.

The golem charged them. The massive creature was only a few yards away when Tomas grabbed Pete's arm and jumped. Because they were holding a weapon with a custos, they easily jumped right over the giant. The golem turned around, roared, and then put its two rock hands together.

"Get out of the way!" roared Pete, and he and Tomas both leaped to the side. Once they were out of the way, the golem shot a crystal out of one of its hands. Officer Hellmount was so busy looking at Pete that he never saw the crystal coming. The crystal went right through Officer Hellmount and into the generator behind Pete. The Officer looked down at his chest where the crystal had hit him, back up at the golem, and then at Tomas and Pete.

"Peter, how did you know?" Officer Hellmount asked in a shaky voice.

"Didn't," Pete said. "It's called dumb luck."

Suddenly, Hellmount turned back into his true form. He looked like a normal man, but his entire body was the color of the solar system—not cosmic latte but a purplish-blue with small white dots that represented stars.

Tomas's jaw dropped. It was the true form of darkness.

"Don't survive," the officer said, speaking his last words. Then he dissolved, just like Allen had done while playing Capture the Flag.

"Tomas," Pete said, "you know I'm not going to make it to tomorrow, don't you?"

"What? Why?" Tomas said.

"Weren't you listening? Dondo said something about a fool going into the sod. Sod is the surface, the ground. I'm going to die today, Tomas. If I choose to survive, the universe will die. Prophecies all link to the existence of the universe. I just want you to know that your father has given up his search for you and is now back at his home on Hera. You are—"

Tomas never got to hear the rest of what Pete was going to say, because there was a loud crash below them. Tomas looked over the side of the wide platform he was standing on and saw *The Winter* firing at the generator. Then he looked over at Pete, who was dangling over the edge of the platform. The shock had sent him flying back.

"Pete!" Tomas said, running over to him. The golem was recharging, but it wasn't moving. Tomas knelt down at the railing and offered to help Pete, but instead Pete just asked a question.

"Tomas, do you think that if I die this day, I will die a hero?"

"Definitely," Tomas assured him.

Pete smiled, and then he let go of the railing and fell. He just missed *The Winter* by a few feet and fell all the way back to Morinthia.

Pete was gone forever this time.

CHAPTER 8
The Battle of Morinthia

Tomas sat there for at least a minute, just staring down at the surface of Morinthia. *The Winter* had noticed him and stopped firing. Tomas got up and walked toward the landing platform. He opened the door and looked around for his craft, but he couldn't find it anywhere. He also couldn't find Mr. Gaffen, who had probably died.

Tomas walked over to the edge of the platform and looked around. His ship was nowhere in sight. Then *The Winter* came up from under the warship and landed on the other side of the landing platform.

Tomas walked over to it with his head down and went aboard. Everyone was looking at him nervously. "Sorry, Tomas. We didn't know who he was," Amber said, rubbing the back of her neck and looking down. They all stood there for a few moments in silence, but the silence was broken by the sound of rock against metal. They all looked out of the ship and saw the golem charging them.

"Close the door!" Roger yelled. The ship took off, leaving only the golem on the landing platform. Tomas thought that was the end of it, but the golem jumped up from the edge and went soaring up into the air, almost as if it were flying.

As they landed back on the surface of Morinthia, this time closer to the battle, they saw something emerge from the not-so-distant fuel shack: peacekeepers.

"Let's burn them to ash," Teddy said, putting his fist into his hand.

"Why not?" Tomas said. "Wait? Valery, did you destroy the warship?"

"I shot Teddy's time bomb onto the generator," Valery said. "The bomb made destroying the ship easy." As they walked out of *The Winter*, they saw pieces of debris from the warship falling from the sky. They headed toward the battle between the Nebula Corps, Checks, and peacekeepers.

"I wonder what's happening in my school?" Tomas said to himself. He had gone to school for most of his life, but over vacation he had gone on the journey with his father to Frozer.

As they approached the battle, Tomas noticed that Teddy was falling behind. He had a limp. Tomas slowed down and waited for him. "What's the matter?" Tomas asked. "While I was running, I tripped on a rock and sprained my foot, I think," Teddy said.

"You should stay here," Tomas said. "Go and hide behind one of those rocks." He pointed to some boulders. Teddy limped over to them and sat down behind one of the larger ones.

Tomas caught up with the rest of the group and got his ax ready. Amber got her blasters ready. Roger put on some brass knuckles and drew his sword. Valery drew her sword and got her other hand in position to be ready to snap. Allen had left his sword behind because he had his power. Patrick waved the wooden plank attached to his shoulder. They definitely weren't ready for a full-out war.

Sergeant Wilson should have seen it coming. He should have known Mr. Gaffen would be back. But the sergeant had thought Gaffen's disappearance meant that he had died.

Instead Gaffen had somehow gotten hold of a Nebula Corps craft and had flown it off the massive warship only moments before it had blown up in flames. And now he was back.

Sergeant Wilson's forehead was now bandaged after being hit by the strange spell that Mr. Gaffen had shot at him from his sword, and he headed outside for a closer view of his enemy.

"Missed me already, have you?" the sergeant asked.

"I've come to reclaim something of mine," Mr. Gaffen said.

"I have nothing that belongs to you," Sergeant Wilson said bitterly.

"But you do," Mr. Gaffen said happily with a smirk.

"What is it?"

"Do you work for Madam Pofer?" Gaffen asked.

"I do," the sergeant said.

"Then you will not mind if I kill her."

"Why?"

"Without her, the Nebula Guard will fall."

Sergeant Wilson didn't know what Gaffen was talking about, but he took out a blaster and fired at him. His shot hit its target, and surprisingly, Mr. Gaffen fell, gasping. During Gaffen's last few moments alive, Wilson knelt over him with a frown.

"Fool!" Mr. Gaffen said with a smile. "A war is fought with weapons, but it is won with something else." And then he died.

Sergeant Wilson stood up and brushed himself off. He walked away, not thinking about the solar lord's last words. As he put his helmet back on, he gathered the most powerful weapons he could find. "I believe this war can be won with weapons," he said.

Tomas and the others all shot lasers, beams of light, or jet-colored rocks at the peacekeepers and Queen-4430s. As the battle raged on, Tomas couldn't find any of his companions anywhere. Nebula Corps troopers and peacekeepers swarmed him. He decided to keep on fighting.

The Nebula Corps was winning, and the peacekeepers' numbers diminished as they were forced back into the destroyed fuel shack. Tomas's hopes were high, until he saw a peacekeeper coming out of the shack and looking frantically around. It was Azamore, and he noticed Tomas. His golden sword and cloak glimmered in the light of day. He slowly walked down to where Tomas was, not seeming to notice the mayhem all around him.

Tomas wanted to run, but he couldn't force himself to do it. He just stood with his mouth slightly ajar. Then he ran up to Azamore, and the two clashed their weapons for what seemed like forever. Then Tomas did what he had done with the space pirate back at the academy. He hadn't known what to do back then, but his mind had told him to do one thing, and he had done it without thinking.

Tomas jumped up and did a full spin, holding his ax in front of him. He hit Azamore, but he never knew exactly where. All he knew was that he penetrated Azamore's armor and heard something shatter. Then the peacekeeper's bones turned gray.

When Tomas looked at him, Azamore was staring back. "This war cannot be won with weapons but with heart," Azamore said, "and you have lots of it. Good luck." And then he turned to dust and blew away with the wind.

"Tomas," someone called from behind him. Tomas turned around to see who it was, and there was Valery with a look of sorrow in her eyes. "Roger, Patrick, and Teddy wouldn't go down without a fight," she said, running over to Tomas and hugging him.

"Wait, Teddy had a sprained ankle," Tomas said.

"He pulled the same trick that Roger pulled on you back at the academy," Valery said, laughing and crying at the same time.

As he was hugging her, Tomas looked up and saw a massive rock hurtling toward the ground. It was the golem. "I have one last job to finish," Tomas said.

Holding his ax, he jumped high and landed on the golem while it was about three hundred feet from the ground. Once he got a good grip on it, he held the golem with one hand and brought up the other hand with the ax in it. He brought the ax down as hard as he could.

The golem yelled a hearty roar, and then Tomas hit the ground.

CHAPTER 9
The Defining Moments

Valery screamed when the golem hit the ground. Dust and bits of rock flew everywhere, leaving a massive crater. Everyone waited for what was going to happen next. Even the Queen-4430s stopped attacking and watched. People on the ground started moving back in case the golem still lived, which it would have if it had hit the ground without Tomas striking it.

Allen came over to the crater, and so did Amber. Then a shadow emerged from the dust cloud. It was Tomas. He had cuts and gashes all over his body, and in some parts, he had bits of rock. He looked around at the mass of people looking at him. Then all the peacekeepers vanished, just like Azamore. Tomas didn't know why, but he gave a half smile. The Check ships all turned around and headed out to space.

A few days later, Tomas and his remaining companions ended up on Hera. Tomas didn't know why they were on Hera, but Valery had decided she wanted to go there. Tomas still had many unanswered questions, but he decided to keep them to himself. Soon they were setting up sleeping bags under the stars in the middle of the woods.

Then Tomas remembered what Pete had said about his father being back on Hera. He walked over to the others, who were telling ghost stories. "Guys, with you I have had the adventure of a lifetime. Mine ended only a few hours ago, but yours is just beginning. Go off and make a change. There is still danger out there—and evil. Go and make the solar system a better place to live in."

They did not reply but just watched. "Tomas, will we ever see you again?" Allen asked.

"It's not my job to ensure that you will," Tomas said. "We must all take life one step at a time."

"Good-bye, Tomas Knight," Valery said. She ran over and hugged him. "Your name will spread hope across the galaxy forever."

Then Tomas ran off into the woods. He walked a few miles alone, and then he saw it: a large barn with a small cottage next to it. He heard a dog barking. It was his home.

The sun was rising now, making the world seem a brilliant orange. As Tomas got closer, he saw a man come out the front door of the cottage.

"Tomas?" the man said. "Tomas! Is that really you?"

"Dad!" Tomas said, and he ran into his father's arms.

The dog jumped up on Tomas. "Henry!" Tomas said, kneeling down and petting his dog.

"What happened?" his father asked.

And Tomas replied with joy, "Oh, do I have a story for you."

EPILOGUE

The next morning, Tomas walked outside to see something fly over the tops of the trees. On the side of it was a name that would spread hope all across the galaxy: *Winter*.

Tomas never did see his friends again. The Check Army never did fall, but it was weakened. Tomas later learned that Dondo had written two prophecies, one revolving around Tomas, and another revolving around his son. The prophecy stated that with every ending came a new beginning.

But Tomas Knight himself would never forget the story of *The Winter*.

ABOUT THE AUTHOR

Benjamin Sturdy began writing science fiction stories at the age of seven. When not writing science fiction novels, Benjamin enjoys hiking and exploring the coast and woodlands near his home in Massachusetts. He lives with his family and dog.

Printed in the United States
By Bookmasters